RAVEN'S BLOOD

RAVEN'S BLOOD

Gil Burgess

authorHOUSE®

AuthorHouse™ LLC
1663 Liberty Drive
Bloomington, IN 47403
www.authorhouse.com
Phone: 1-800-839-8640

Published by AuthorHouse   06/12/2014

ISBN: 978-1-4969-1625-9 (sc)
ISBN: 978-1-4969-1659-4 (e)

Library of Congress Control Number: 2014909778

CHAPTER I

THURSDAY MORNING, MAY 24th
New Hope, Pennsylvania

The early morning stillness of Raven Hall found new owner Chris Donnely meandering along the newly laid paver pathway down from the main building to the cabana and pool area. He stopped periodically to pinch off dead blooms from the red Knock Out roses that lined the walk. He and his life partner, Dave Taylor, had purchased the facility last fall and had spent the long winter months refurbishing the somewhat run-down resort; updating the dozen guest rooms, the dining room and pool and cabana area all in preparation for this, their first summer season. "I hope to God we do well," Chris muttered as he tossed the spent blooms into the nearby trash can and surveyed the pool for anything else that might need his attention.

His main concern was, as usual, financial. He'd spent many sleepless nights worrying about paying for the substantial loans, the never-ending stream of supplies, as well as meeting the rather large payroll.

1

"It'll be okay," Dave had reassured him, "We'll be fine! Don't worry." But no matter how many times he had heard those words Chris still worried.

He stood at the wrought iron gate that separated the pool area from the newly expanded porch, his flaxen hair lifting in the early morning breeze, and surveyed the freshly planted white wave petunias that were already cascading down the sides of the antiqued planters rimming the patio of the pool area. Standing in the center of each of the planters was a vivid yellow hibiscus, creating a colorful contrast to the dark needles of fifty-plus-year old stand of white pines that bordered the property along the Bridge Street side. The early morning summer sun glinted off the crystal clear water that lapped against the sides of the in-ground pool, bouncing beams of brightness into the rapidly warming air. Chris stopped and took in the scene, sipping his morning coffee. Everything seemed perfect and he let himself relax, almost.

He had to laugh when he remembered the condition of the resort when he and Dave first laid eyes on it. His immediate response was to put on his best Bette Davis imitation, "What a dump!"

The main building and the guest twelve rooms that formed the foundation of the resort were structurally sound but in need of a good cleaning and modernization. Fresh paint, new carpeting and bedding and updated fixtures in the bathrooms did the trick for the guest rooms while a deep cleaning of the elaborate carved paneling and replacement of the carpeting in the dining room, main bar and Oak Room piano bar gave those neglected spaces a new life.

The covered cedar patio that fronted the main bar hadn't existed then and was an item he and Dave had many heated discussions about adding on. Now he was grateful he had given in. It added a much needed indoor/outdoor space with its vaulted ceiling and large windows with views of the pool and cabana beyond.

The pool had been empty and left uncovered for several seasons and needed to be emptied of debris and dead creatures before the resurfacing and restoration could even begin. With that complete, the small restroom and shower behind the cabana bar were renovated. He, Dave and a constant stream of plumbers, electricians and contractors had labored for almost a year creating what he now looked out onto.

Starting back up the pathway he muttered, "I hope it was all worth it!"

A sudden shout jolted him back to the here and now. He turned to see Dave gesturing for him, his normally handsome face even more so in the low angled sunlight. At first he smiled, but then his stomach knotted and his worries returned. *Something's wrong*, he thought as he tossed the remaining now cold coffee out and raced to the office where Dave had retreated to. Panting, he asked, "What's wrong?"

Dave leaned back in his chair and grinned. "Dave! What's wrong?"

Dave shook his head and laughed, "Come here."

As Chris hesitantly approached he stood and took his lover in his arms, "What have I been telling you for months now?"

"Turn over and stop snoring?"

"No, silly. To relax, that everything would be okay."

"Yeah, and?"

Dave leaned over and picked up the reservation book. "We're booked solid from now straight through to the end of July! Looks like Raven Hall is a success!"

Chris' knees weakened and he felt lightheaded, he could not believe what he was hearing. "Seriously?"

Tossing the book back onto the table, Dave nodded. "Now will you please relax!"

"I think I need to sit down before I fall down." He exhaled the breath he didn't know he was holding and slumped into the nearest chair.

Dave started to speak again, but Chris silenced him with his hand held up. "Whoa, let this sink in for a moment." He took a deep breath and exhaled. "Ah," he sighed as he snuggled deeply into the plush leather chair. For the first time since their adventure started almost ten months ago he felt the tension in his body ease. Everything appeared to be going their way.

~ ~ ~

Lincroft, New Jersey

Brett Anders scanned his overfilled closet and checked the disorderly dresser drawers searching for anything he might have overlooked. He glanced over at the pile of clothing strewn on his double bed and laughed aloud, "What the hell am I doing?" he asked himself. There was more than enough heaped on the unmade bed for a week's vacation, let alone a long weekend. He closed the closet doors, shut the dresser drawers and started sorting the items into two piles; one definitely, the other maybe. He whittled the mound down to a reasonable amount and began folding and placing the definite pile into his black nylon bag. With those items packed he discovered he had only room enough left for his toiletries. "Well, I guess my packing is done!" he commented as he stared at the bulging bag.

Glancing into the full length mirror on the closet door, he chided himself, "I should have gone on a diet." Brett was never quite satisfied with his appearance, although he was tall, thin and very handsome. His fair complexion and crystal blue eyes were gifts from his mother's side of the family while his ability to eat and not gain weight came from his dad. "Oh well, I guess what I see is what I get!"

This would be the first time he was to go away since he and Alan split up last October. That sudden realization hit him like a sucker punch to the gut. He could feel his eyes welling up but refused to give in to that raw emotion. He could still remember the night Alan told him it was over.

"I can't do this any longer. I feel like I'm living a lie," he'd said in a calm and controlled voice, his eyes downcast, staring at his intertwined fingers. Brett had sat, icy coldness seeping into his veins. He wanted to speak, but his throat was dry and his mouth refused to form any words.

"I need to be by myself, away from this town, my job and even the people I work with and," he looked into Brett's crystal blue eyes, "and you."

Brett felt as if the breath had suddenly been sucked out of him. His mouth dropped open and his hands began to tremble. "Where is this coming from?" he asked, his voice returning.

"It's been coming for some time now, I'm afraid." Alan rose and started pacing the living room in their Lincroft apartment. "I don't know when or even how it started, all I know is that something isn't working for me any longer and I need to sort things out, alone."

Brett stood and faced him. "Sort things out? You mean us."

Alan nodded.

The room grew heavy with silence as Brett tried to take in what he'd just heard from his lover of the past three years. His mind swirled with confusion as he tried to make sense of what he'd just heard. There had been no clue, no hint of anything wrong between the two of them. "Is there someone else?" Brett asked, terrified of the response.

"No."

"Then this is all within you. You aren't happy with me, with this town, with your job, with yourself." Brett sat at the edge of the sofa.

Alan shrugged, "That about sums it up." He returned to the sofa and sat close to Brett, taking his hands in his. "Please understand that I need to do this."

Brett pulled his hands away and stood, staring out the picture window, "No, you need help. See a doctor, a therapist. You can't just run from all this because wherever you go the problems you have will be there, waiting for you."

Alan rose and started towards the door. "Maybe, but right now I have to go. I have to be alone, someplace different." And with that he was gone, the door closing softly after him. Brett stood shocked for a long moment, hugging himself against a sudden chill. His eyes absently turned from the closed door to the window and stared down at the busy street. He couldn't believe what he saw; there was Alan getting into a car with another man. Brett stared in shock as he watched the man he'd lived with for the past two years and planned to spend the rest of his life with lean over and kiss this stranger.

Brett's blood ran cold as he suddenly realized that he'd been played. "That son of a bitch!" he sputtered. He stared as the black SUV pulled away from the curb, wanting to run after it and confront Alan, but that wasn't necessary now; he had the truth. He simply watched the vehicle blend into the afternoon traffic.

Brett sighed deeply as that painful night six months ago replayed in his mind. He grabbed the bag and placed it near the door. He'd put it in the car in the morning so he could get an early start. He wondered what the Memorial Day weekend would hold for him; maybe new friends, new experiences and maybe even a new love. It would hold more than he could imagine.

~ ~ ~

THURSDAY EVENING
New Hope, Pennsylvania

Chief Medical Examiner for Bucks County, Dr. Driscoll sat at his cluttered desk filing reports and signing death certificates. As Chief M.E. there was always paperwork; a report to write, forms to fill out, police reports to complete even when there were no autopsies to perform.

Tossing his reading glasses onto the pile of clutter on his desk he leaned back and rubbed his irritated eyes. Stretching and yawning, he glanced at the wall clock above his office door. It was already nearing 7 P.M. He snatched up the phone and called his wife to tell her he would be late. She sighed and gruffly replied, "Okay," and hung up. Grabbing his briefcase he checked to be sure he hadn't forgotten anything. Smiling wryly he turned out the lights and headed out, there was something he needed to do before heading home to her.

~ ~ ~

Chris spent the remainder of that day in a state of bliss. Hearing that they were booked through to the end of July helped to alleviate most of his fears, but there was still a little irritating gnawing in the pit of his stomach that kept him from becoming too complacent. He stood at the edge of the pool, his favorite spot in the resort, taking in deep breaths of the cooled late spring air. As the sun began to set in the west, Dave sidled up behind him, "Hey you," he said as he wrapped his arms around Chris's waist. "You haven't eaten all day, you must be hungry."

"Not really. Let's just stay here and watch the sun set."

Leading him to one of the lounge chairs, Dave sat and pulled Chris down in front of him. He kissed his neck and held him close. "I don't want you to worry. I told you everything was going to be okay."

"I know. I should have listened to you." Chris turned to face Dave, his eyes dark and deep in the dimming sunlight. He kissed him and leaned onto his chest, listening to the steady beat of his heart. "Thank you for putting up with me for the past several months."

Dave kissed his forehead, "What choice did I have? When you love somebody you have to be there for them, no matter what."

Chris smiled, "Thanks."

Sitting up and back, Dave continued, "I do have to admit, though, that there were times I wanted to strangle you." He laughed. "Come on, I need to eat and I can hear your stomach growling."

Chris rose and pulled Dave up into a warm embrace and sighed. This was good.

~ ~ ~

Dr. Driscoll made the purchases he needed at the local pharmacy. He folded the plastic CVS bag neatly and placed it in the dark recesses of the trunk of his car. He couldn't help but grin as he thought of what the next few days could bring. He'd waited most of the long, snowy winter to be able to act upon his desires, now finally they'd be realized. He started the car and instead of heading home made another stop at Havana's for a few drinks. His relationship with his wife of eleven years had become increasingly strained as the demands of his job increased. He had tried to be patient with her growing frustration, but after many months of trying to appease her he gave up and started developing his own life away from the marriage. That was when he hired Emily Hargrove, a young, attractive assistant eager to learn from and please him. He downed three scotch and sodas and sighing heavily headed home. Remembering what was in the trunk and what it could bring, he smiled, confident that he would soon have what he wanted.

~ ~ ~

Lincroft, New Jersey

The packing done, Brett turned his attention to having dinner. He didn't want to cook, it was late already, and he was hungry. Eating fast food was out of the question, he couldn't remember the last time he was in a McDonald's or a Burger King. He called Pamela, one of his oldest friends, and asked her to meet him at the Lincroft Inn. She had already eaten but agreed to meet him for a drink. He hung up and grabbed his jacket and keys.

As he drove the short distance to the Inn, he kept thinking of the depressing turn of events that had led him to this place in his life. He could still see Alan with that other man and even these many months later that vision still caused him to flush with anger.

After being seated he ordered a glass of pinot noir and read over the menu. Dining alone was something he'd have to get accustomed to and he found it a bit unnerving. He felt like the other diners as well as the wait staff were staring at him, commenting about his lack of a dinner companion. He raised the menu to cover his face more than to peruse the selections. After ordering he sat back and sipped the deeply satisfying wine. He and Alan had had their first date here and he smiled at that memory. They dated for several months before making a commitment to each other. *Huh*, he thought, *I guess his commitment had an expiration date*. He smirked as the waitress brought his caesar salad. As he began eating, enjoying the richness of the dressing and the crisp romaine and croutons, Pamela arrived. "Hey", she started as she plopped into the cushioned seat across from him, "You all packed?"

Brett nodded.

"How many suitcases?" she chided, knowing that he'd probably over packed.

"Only one, Missy!"

"Wow! That's a record for you."

Brett grinned, "It's a new me!"

"Great to heat that. Now," she scanned the room for a server, "Who do you have to screw to get a drink in this joint?"

As Brett continued eating and Pamela sipped her dirty martini, their conversation turned to the upcoming holiday weekend. "Maybe this weekend will start the next stage of life for me," Brett muttered.

Pamela nodded, "Good for you! Forget that cheating son of a bitch. You deserve better." She toasted him with her second drink, "Here's to a new beginning."

Brett hoped she was right.

He returned home still feeling a bit depressed, but better. Pamela always put things into perspective in her own unique way. Tossing his keys on the living room coffee table, Brett plopped onto the sofa and clicked on the television. He saw the images moving on the screen, heard the dialog of the characters and the laughter of the audience, but nothing registered, he stared blankly into space. He shortly found himself nodding off and decided to turn in early. On his way to the bedroom he stopped and stared at the packed suitcase near the door. "Hopes for a new beginning," he silently said aloud, "If only..." He made his way to the bed and fell onto the comforter. He kicked off his sneakers and tossed his jeans and shirt into the corner. Sliding under the sheets he sighed heavily. *Why couldn't I find someone else?* He thought. *What's wrong with me?* He fell into a heavy, alcohol induced slumber but slept fitfully, snippets of dreams troubling him throughout the long night.

CHAPTER II

FRIDAY MORNING, MAY 25th
Lincroft, New Jersey

Brett woke while it was still dark. He tried to let his body get more of the rest it desperately needed, but it was no use. He tried to focus on the alarm clock on his nightstand, blinking and rubbing the crusty sleep out of his eyes, "Five A.M.!" He flopped back onto the rumpled sleep-warmed sheets and closed his eyes. Suddenly he sat up bolt straight in bed. The sun was rising and he glanced over to see it was nearing 7:30. "Damn it!" He'd slipped back into a deep sleep and never heard the alarm clock, but then remembered it hadn't been set; he'd taken the day off. He fell back and let his body drift away again, before he finally got up. He leisurely went through his morning routine and made a wholesome breakfast. By 10:00 he'd straightened up the apartment and was ready to leave. He grabbed his keys and with one final scan of his home, grabbed the case and was out the door.

Although it was about a two-hour drive from his Lincroft home, he wanted to enjoy the scenery along the ride through rural New Jersey, maybe stop in the town of New Hope and do some window shopping before checking in at The Raven. He allowed his mind to wander as he negotiated the winding country roads leading to the

Delaware River. The early-spring freshness of the foliage, the clusters of daffodils, flowering dogwood trees and the lush green grass excited him into a euphoric state. *Maybe I will meet someone new this weekend,* he thought, then laughed at his optimism. He didn't want a one-night stand, but wouldn't be opposed to one either. But more than anything, he wanted the security and support of a lasting relationship, something that he thought he'd found with Alan. He wondered if it could happen again. He wasn't sure, but was determined to find out.

~ ~ ~

New Hope, Pennsylvania

As the sun rose higher and guests started arriving, Chris' worries began escalating again. His mind jumbled with thoughts such as, *Will the guests like the newly refurbished rooms? Will the meals be well prepared and served in a timely manner and hot? How about the servers? The bartenders? Housekeeping?* and so on. Watching the staff at work he found himself picking at his lip, his attention now focused on making sure they were doing their jobs correctly. Dave came up behind him and whispered, "Hey, come on, I'll buy you breakfast."

Still watching the check in, Chris shook his head, "Not now."

"Chris, come on! Let the staff we hired do the jobs we pay them for!"

Chris sighed, "You're right." He turned to face Dave, "I actually am hungry."

Little did they know their peaceful resort would soon be thrown into chaos.

~ ~ ~

FRIDAY AFTERNOON
Lambertville, New Jersey

Brett turned onto the Bridge Street in the historic town of Lambertville, New Jersey, around noon. He was anxious to get to The Raven, the name Raven Hall had come to be known by, but needed to get out and stretch his legs for a while. The drive was a little more stressful than he expected due to road construction on Route 29. He managed to find a parking space a block off the main drag and took a leisurely stroll up and down the narrow streets, window shopping. The sun felt good on his skin and he deeply inhaled the warm spring air. A wave of calm washed over him and for the first time in a long time he felt at peace with himself and his life. He was no longer anxious about meeting someone, he was content. "This is good," he said aloud as he returned to his car for the last few minutes of the drive.

Crossing over the Delaware River into New Hope was like going back in time. The buildings, many dating back to the pre-Civil War era, were a collection of brick, clapboard and Pennsylvania stone crowded together and almost touching the blacktopped street. The side streets wound around each other, some doubling back to the main road, others leading out of the town and up through the rolling hills of eastern Pennsylvania, but instead of heading straight to The Raven, he travelled north. The topography here rose and the roads twisted even more. Revolutionary War construction was evident, many of the buildings, both private and public, boasted "Circa" plaques. He marveled at the sturdiness of these buildings, knowing that they had stood the test of time, something many of today's structures would be hard pressed to do. Finally, he turned the car around and made his way to The Raven, still lost in his euphoria.

~ ~ ~

New Hope, Pennsylvania

After yet another heated argument with Adriana the previous evening, Dr. Driscoll lost himself in his work. True, he had a very capable assistant, but he needed to be hands on today. As he worked he replayed the events of the previous evening and the more he thought about them the angrier he became. Adriana had become so distant over the past few months and he knew his promotion to Chief Medical Examiner had put a strain on their relationship, but it seemed to him that her attitude, anger and outright hostility at times were unjustified. He'd given up on the thought that she'd adjust to his new job and its demands and had started staying away from home longer and longer each day, sometimes until he was certain she was asleep. He had started harboring angry and violent thoughts that frightened him at first, but which grew each time they'd had another argument. He knew he could never do harm to her, but letting his mind play out various scenarios of doing just that seemed to appease his growing anger, and served to calm him.

~ ~ ~

Brett arrived at Raven Hall around four, just in time for happy hour to begin. He wasn't surprised to find the main parking lot filled but managed to squeeze his Hyundai Sonata into the lot near the street. He left his bag in the trunk and headed into the main lobby to register. He elbowed and excused his way through the growing throngs of men on the patio and finally made it to the registration area. After getting his room key he retrieved his bag and followed the receptionist's directions to his room, which was located down a flight of steep stairs and to the left of the main building. "I sure hope this path is lit at night!" he muttered as he hefted his nylon bag over his shoulder and carefully made his way down the stairs. He took one more look around before opening the room's door; the isolated location and darkness unnerved him, but he shrugged it off.

The room was bright and well appointed. There was a double bed, flanked by two nightstands. A small table and side chairs, as well as a coffee maker had been placed in front of the large picture window, and the carpeting under his feet was deep and plush. It was obvious that the room had recently been redecorated and painted. He smiled as he hoisted his bag onto the bed and started unpacking. He once again allowed his mind to wander to thoughts of meeting someone. He showered and dressed in his favorite faded jeans, the ones that hugged him in all the right places, and a just-tight-enough white button-down shirt. Once he slipped on his Dockers, he surveyed his look in the mirror. "Not bad," he said with a smile, "Not bad at all." Like many of his generation, Brett worked hard at keeping fit. He worked out four to five times a week and watched his diet religiously. This weekend, however he'd splurge; forget the diet and let his guard down, maybe even give in to meaningless sex with a stranger. He laughed at that last thought, he had rarely done that, but being here with so many available men might be the perfect opportunity to let loose his primal urges. With one more glance in the mirror he picked up his room key and left to see what was available.

~ ~ ~

FRIDAY EVENING

Mike, a local and rare visitor to Raven Hall slid his car into a parking spot in the shadows. Killing the engine and lights he sat motionless watching the comings and goings of the crowds of men, hearing their laughter and seeing them touch each other. His excitement grew as he spied one couple making out. He stared intently at them, watching their hands glide over each other's lean bodies, caressing and groping, hips thrusting, butts clenching, moving in unison. Unable to contain his arousal his hand slid down and unzipped his slacks, he reached in and stroked faster and faster, never taking his eyes off the two men. Finally, feeling the imminent heaving of orgasm he increased his stroking and, with his free hand, reached up and pinched his nipples hard, wincing as the pain of the pinching and the pleasure of release coursed through his body simultaneously. He zipped up his trousers, sat back and grinned, the tension released, his body and mind calm. The two men had gone, but they'd fulfilled their purpose. He sat for a moment longer, letting his breathing return to normal, then started his car and slowly backed out of the parking spot and headed home.

His desire for male sex had intensified over the past several months. In his younger years he'd experienced the intense pleasure of man-to-man sex, but fought to squelch the desire as he grew older. Once an adult he hoped those erotic feelings would be eradicated for good and for many years they were. But now, for some unknown reason, he found those old lustful urges rearing themselves again and growing more intense as time went by. His visits to the shadowy parking lot at Raven Hall had become more frequent, and his fantasies darker and tinged with sadomasochistic desires.

He'd yet to physically act out any of his needs, but knew it wouldn't be long before he'd have to act on them, to feel another man, take him, use him then toss him away. On the ride home he let his mind wander to many erotic scenarios and grinned. No, it wouldn't be long now, maybe even this weekend.

~ ~ ~

Brett stood at the patio bar sipping a coke, waiting for his table to be ready. He wanted a drink, but had opted not to have one until after he'd eaten. He scanned the spacious patio. Everywhere he looked there were small groups of men talking or sharing a laugh. It seemed to him that he was the only person at the resort who was alone and he began to feel uncomfortable. His eyes shifted to the long narrow indoor bar that opened onto the patio and slowly made his way to the shadowy interior space. He remembered what it felt like to be part of a couple, to belong to someone special and the hurt began to mushroom inside him. It didn't, however, have a chance to fully blossom, as he was beckoned by a rather swishy young host, "Mr. Anders, your table is ready. Follow me please." Brett dutifully trailed behind through the crowded bar. Once in the open hallway he was informed that due to the overwhelming crowd the management had taken the liberty of seating another single guest with him; if he approved of course. Brett's spirits immediately lifted; he wasn't the only one here alone. "That's fine," he replied, "I hate eating alone."

As they neared the table on the upper level of the two tiered dining room a tall, dark haired man stood and extended his hand. Brett grinned widely, he had hoped his dinner mate would be young and attractive and he was that and more; he was hot! The host introduced the two men and Brett could swear he saw a sly grin appear on the man's face. This was going to be a dinner to remember.

After the host left the table to see to other guests Brett and his dinner companion, who introduced himself as Anthony D'Angelo, immediately fell into easy conversation. Anthony hailed from Brooklyn, was 32, and worked on Wall Street for Bank of America.

Brett's thoughts instantly turned to the events of 9/11. "Were you there when it happened?" he asked in a hushed voice.

Anthony nodded and his face paled. Brett could see the sadness in his eyes.

"I'm sorry, I shouldn't have said anything."

Anthony looked up, directly into Brett's deep blue eyes, "That's okay," he reassured him in a shaky voice.

Brett reached across the small table and took Anthony's hands in his. Anthony squeezed his hands in response and smiled, "Thanks, that feels good."

The host, having noticed the hand holding and the way the two men looked at each other smiled and sighed, "I'm such a yenta!"

Brett and Anthony spent the next two hours in relaxed conversation, enjoying not only their meals and wine, but each other's company. After coffee was served and the check paid Brett felt awkward. He didn't want the evening to end so abruptly.

As they stood and started leaving the dining room, Anthony took Brett's hand in his, "So, Brett, what now?"

Brett grinned, "Whatever you want." Seeing the gleam in Anthony's eyes Brett immediately knew he'd said the wrong thing. He started to qualify his comment when Anthony put a finger to his lips. "Come on, let's get a drink and go sit by the pool."

~ ~ ~

It wasn't until well after midnight that the dining room had emptied and the staff could get down to the business of clearing, cleaning and setting the tables for the morning breakfast. Craig Jamison, the dining room manager, stretched and rubbed his aching back, "God I'm tired and my feet! They'll never be the same after tonight."

"You'd better get used to it," Dave told him as he and Chris helped the exhausted staff clean, "I've got a strong feeling the whole season is going to be like this."

"Well," he moaned as he massaged the back of his neck, "It'll all be worth it as long as the tips are like this!" He waved a stack of bills like a fan, then rolled it up and stuffed it into his slacks.

"Don't expect that every day," Dave warned him. Looking around the room he was satisfied. "I'm off to bed." He turned to Craig, "You working breakfast?"

"Yeah, but I'm too wound up to sleep." He eyed the patio and the cabana bar beyond it. "I'm going to play for a while."

Dave shook his head, "Don't stay out too late and for God's sake be careful!" With that he took Chris's hand and they left for their private quarters, knowing that if any crisis arose the general manager would be able to handle it quickly.

Craig shot him a sidelong glance, "No, Dad, I won't stay out too late," and raising his right hand as if swearing on a Bible he concluded, "And I promise to be careful." Smiling, he strode off into the crowd, his senses and libido raging for action.

~ ~ ~

Brett and Anthony lounged side by side at the edge of the resort's pool. Although the pool wasn't large enough to actually swim in the crystal clear water would offer cooling relief from the upcoming summer's heat and humidity. The two men sat quietly for a while enjoying the cool night air and simply being together. The entire resort echoed with the voices and laughter of the hundreds of men, some guests, some locals that crowded the patio, pool and cabana bars, but Brett didn't really hear anything; for the first time in a long time was right in the moment. He felt a warmth he'd nearly forgotten and responded to the sensation by moving onto Anthony's lounge chair and running his fingers through his dark brown hair.

"That feels good," Anthony whispered, his eyes closed, enjoying Brett's touch. "Can I ask you something?"

"Sure," Brett responded, pulling himself into a more upright position.

"Why is someone like you still single?"

Brett responded by turning away, a twinge of pain making him unable to answer.

"I'm sorry, I didn't mean to upset you. Forget I asked."

"That's okay," Brett smiled and decided to tell him the entire story.

~ ~ ~

Feeling invigorated by the crowd, the noise, music and the crisp spring air Craig got a vodka and cranberry and scoped out the men. There were so many he could barely tell where one ended and another began. *"Just what I like!"* he thought aloud, *"wall to wall man meat!"* Although the dinner shift had been non-stop running to serve the many attractive guests staying at the resort, the smoothness of the Grey Goose began to relax his mind and body, and his eyes began hunting; his libido at its peak. To his disappointment, almost all of the men appeared to either be with someone or not to his liking.

He side-stepped his way through the body-to-body room out through the patio to the cabana which was full but not as packed as the other bar. It wasn't too long before his eyes locked on a man who appeared to be staring at him. *Not bad,* he thought and smiled. The dark-haired stranger smiled in return. Craig's body was already responding to what his mind envisioned as he approached the man. He checked him out from head to toe, liking what he saw- at least six feet tall, thin, clean shaven with dark hooded eyes.

"Hey," he greeted the stranger, trying to hide his quite visible excitement.

After noticing what Craig was trying to hide the man's smile broadened. He extended his hand, "Mike," he said sharply.

Craig gripped and held onto the large, warm hand for a long moment trying to convey his need. That wasn't necessary as Mike bluntly stated, "Let's get out of here."

Craig gulped the rest of his drink and followed him back through the patio and along the side of the building.

Thinking they were headed to Mike's car then to his place, Craig was quite surprised when Mike led him down the dirt path to a wooded area just east of the boundaries of Raven Hall near Sugan Street.

Craig began to become apprehensive. "Ah, where are we going?"

Mike grinned and rubbed his groin, unzipping his jeans. "Right here."

~ ~ ~

Brett and Anthony sat in silence for a long while, Brett feeling the effects of having had an old wound opened. Finally, Anthony asked, "You okay?"

"Yeah," Brett smiled over at him, "I am now. I guess I shouldn't have reacted that way to your question, but..." he shrugged.

"You don't have to explain, everyone reacts differently to life's ups and downs, and from what you told me that wasn't a minor event. I don't know how I'd react." He leaned over and kissed Brett on the cheek. "It's getting late. We'd better call it a night."

Brett stood and stretched, "What time is it anyway?"

"It's almost 2 A.M."

Both men laughed, neither having realized that many hours that had sped by since they'd met. They walked hand in hand to Anthony's room in the front of the building. Standing outside the door, Brett was unsure of what to do. "Well," he started.

"Yeah, well," Anthony repeated then pulled him close and kissed him. The kiss was warm and full, and Brett could feel his head begin to spin.

Anthony pulled away and stared into Brett's eyes, "Get a good night's sleep, or what left of it. I'll see you in the morning for breakfast."

That statement eased Brett's anxiety. "Sure, good night."

They kissed again and Brett turned away hearing the door to Anthony's room open. He smiled as he made his way along the path to his room behind the main building. Somehow being alone tonight wasn't a bad thing, it told him something about the kind of man Anthony was. He undressed and slid into the cool bedding and drifted off into a restful sleep.

~ ~ ~

Craig began getting nervous; this was not something he'd ever done. He wanted this hot man, needed the sex, but out in the open? That wasn't his style. He stopped then started heading back towards The Raven. Mike grabbed his wrist roughly, "What's the matter? Don't you want this?" He pressed Craig's hand onto his engorged shaft.

"Okay, but let's make this quick. I don't feel comfortable doing this here."

Still holding Craig's hand to his crotch, Mike reached out and grabbed him by the back of his neck and pulled him in for a hot, passionate kiss. While the kiss continued, Mike released Craig's hand and groped him hard, causing Craig to wince. "Hey! Take it easy."

Without responding Mike unzipped and unbuckled Craig's jeans and roughly pulled them down. Craig's erection stood forward and out of his boxers. Mike was on it in seconds. As he stood, knees shaking, Craig pulled Mike's head deeper onto his shaft, rotating his hips as he pushed harder and faster into Mike's hot mouth.

After a while, Mike stood and slid his own jeans to his ankles. Craig dropped onto his knees and swallowed him hungrily. He manipulated himself as he pleasured this hot, sexy man; his apprehensions about sex in the open having been long forgotten. Feeling his own climax nearing, Craig stood and pressed his overheated mouth onto Mike's. Soon they were both moaning and within seconds climaxed almost at the same time.

When his breathing and heart rate returned to normal, Craig reached down and pulled up his jeans; once dressed he looked over at Mike who was just zipping up his pants. "Man, Mike that was great. Thanks."

Mike grinned, but somehow Craig felt a twinge of nervousness when he again looked into his face. He started walking away, but turned when he heard his name being called. Thinking he'd dropped something, he turned. "Yeah."

All he saw was a flash of metal blade in the moonlight; it was the last thing Craig would ever see.

Wiping his prints from the handle of the blade, the blood on the damp grass, Mike casually tossed it over the fence separating the woods from Raven Hall, knowing the undergrowth would quickly cover it up forever. He grinned widely as he made his way back to the resort.

CHAPTER III

EARLY SATURDAY MORNING, May 26th
New Hope, Pennsylvania

Brett woke slowly, rolling over and hugging the cold pillow beside him, wondering what it would have been like to wake next to Anthony. "Maybe tonight," he sighed.

Stretching fully he sat up and checked his watch. "Oh God!" he hollered and rushed into the shower. Once fully bathed he dressed in tan cargo shorts and a tight-fitting black T-shirt. There was a knock on his door as he pulled on his Nikes. Startled by the sudden rapping, he asked who it was.

"Housekeeping. May I clean your room, sir?"

When he opened the door there stood Anthony looking as gorgeous in the sunlight as he did in last night's full moon.

Brett grinned and leaned on the door frame, "Well, good morning sir."

Anthony stepped through the threshold, took Brett in his arms and kissed him. "Now that's how to start a morning, I'd say."

"Are you always this romantic in the morning?"

Anthony shrugged, "Morning, afternoon, evening it doesn't make any difference to me. I'm Italian! We're always ready for some *amore*!" Brett pulled him into the room and kissed him again, this time passionately.

They stood for a long moment in each other's arms, drawing comfort and warmth from each other. Finally Brett leaned back and stared into Anthony's deep brown eyes, "I don't know about you, but I'm ravenous!"

"So am I, but do you mean for food or. . .?"

Brett moved past him to the door, "Food now, other nourishment later." He took Anthony's hand and pulled him out of the room.

The dining room was partially full but there seemed to be an air of tension in the staff. They rushed about hurriedly not stopping to chat with guests as they did last night. As they were seated, Brett noticed that there were only two servers. "They seem to be short-handed this morning."

Pulling the large cloth napkin onto his lap, Anthony commented, "As long as I get my coffee! Did you sleep okay?"

Brett nodded. "You?"

"No, not really. Something kept me awake."

"What was it? Some guys having sex outside your door in the parking lot?"

"No, you!" Brett smiled.

The server approached with a pot of steaming coffee, filled both cups and left the pot. He stood quietly, as he took their orders. As they waited for their food the dining room became quite crowded. "Isn't that one of the owners seating guests?"

Anthony looked around to where Brett was motioning. "Yeah, that's odd. Maybe one of the servers didn't show up."

Neither man gave much more thought to the unusual situation and returned to their coffee and conversation.

~ ~ ~

Dave punched in the latest order on the dining room's computer. His thoughts, however, were not on the guests' orders but on Craig. As he pushed the "send" button, his anger began surfacing. "Where the hell is he?" he muttered and turned to approach another table. As he made his way back through the servers' station to the dining room, Chris appeared at the entrance to the dining room. He motioned "come here" to Dave.

Dave excused himself from the guests whose orders he'd just taken and moved with purpose to Chris. He could tell from the look on his face that Chris was worried; something was wrong. Pulling Dave into the coat room, Chris whispered, "Craig never made it home last night."

"Great, that means he's probably shacked up with the trick he picked up last night!"

"Hold on, there's more. Justin said his car is in the same spot it was in last night."

"So? That means he's probably in one of the guest rooms."

"I don't think so." Chris shook his head. "Almost every room is empty, I just checked with housekeeping."

Dave's anger began to turn to concern. "What do we do?"

Again, Chris shook his head, "I don't know. Wait, I guess. What other choice do we have?" He rubbed his arms to ward of the sudden chill he felt. "I'll call his cell again, but it'll probably go right to voice mail like it did before."

"Keep trying, I'll cover for him." Dave patted Chris on the shoulder reassuringly as he left.

Chris pulled out his phone and hit 'redial'. Something was terribly wrong and he could feel his gut tighten once again.

~ ~ ~

Maria Alvarez rushed through the house, grabbing her purse, keys and light spring jacket. She'd overslept and feared she'd be late for work. "I can't be late, not today," she told her husband as she hurried towards the door of their apartment.

"Don't worry, you have time," he told her. "The bus doesn't come for another twenty minutes."

Normally, he'd drive her, but their 1989 Camry was in the shop for what seemed the thousandth time this year.

As she checked to be sure she had everything she needed her frustration at their financial situation increased. "We need a new car. You've known that for months and yet we still drive around in that piece of crap!"

Bernardo agreed with her, but right now a new vehicle was out of the question. "We will buy a new, or nearly new car soon, I promise." He put his arms around her and kissed her freshly washed hair.

Maria smiled up at him, she couldn't be angry with the man she'd been in love with since childhood. "I know we will." She glanced at her watch. "I have to get going. Let Lena sleep, she woke up in the middle of the night after having a bad dream." And with that she was gone.

She raced to the bus stop at the end of the block and had the exact change ready when it hissed to a stop. Once on board, she exhaled deeply, she'd be on time. Maria got off at the corner of Sugan and West Bridge Streets. Since it was a Saturday, and a holiday weekend, the driver was able to make good time, leaving Maria enough time to grab a coffee at the WaWa on the corner across from Raven Hall.

Dark-roast hazelnut in hand, she crossed the narrow road and took the well-worn short cut through the small wooded area that separated Raven Hall from Sugan Street. Keeping her eyes on the narrow winding path, looking for tree roots, she suddenly came to a stop. There was something there that didn't seem to belong, a small pool of what appeared to be blood. Thinking it was a deer that had been struck by a car and managed to make it this far before succumbing to its injuries she continued on, sipping her coffee while keeping focused on the path, which rose slightly as it neared Raven Hall. Her breath caught in her throat and her legs became leaden when she saw a human body crumpled near a pine tree. Finding the ability to move again she raced up the embankment to the resort, dropping the large coffee as she ran.

Once she neared the walkway at the far end of the resort she began screaming and yelling in Spanish, *"Vengan, rapido! Ayudenme! Un asesinato! Por favor!"*

There were a few guests on the porch and hearing her frantic voice they rushed to her. Thinking at first she'd been hurt they asked if she was okay. Maria pointed in the direction of the wooded lot and again spoke in her native tongue, *"y ahi un cuerpo! Muerto!"* She buried her face in her hands, sobbing.

Hearing the commotion, Chris shoved his phone into his pocket and rushed to outside the her, "What's wrong? What happened?"

The man nearest to him shrugged, "I don't know, she said something in Spanish and pointed to the woods over there."

Chris pushed through the small group, bent down to Maria who immediately grabbed him tightly, still rambling on in Spanish. Chris knew enough of the language to understand the most important words. His head snapped up at the word *"muerto."*. A cold sweat broke onto his brow as he took Maria by the arm, addressing the nearest bystander. "Please do me a favor, take her into the dining room and tell Dave to take her to the office. I'll be there shortly." The stunned man nodded took Maria's shaking hand and led her away.

His throat dry, his breathing staggered, Chris slowly made his way down the back stairs into the wooded grove. Shortly he came to a small pool of blood, his fists clenched tightly and turned to ice. Turning slightly, not wanting to see what caused the blood, but knowing he had to, Chris slowly raised his eyes from the ground level, following the drying fluid to its source. First he saw the feet, then the torso and finally he head, almost severed from the body. "Oh God!" he screamed and slipped on the slick blood. Scurrying back to get to his feet his hands, jeans and even his face became splattered with a mix of mud and blood. Finally regaining his footing, Chris made his way back to the resort.

~ ~ ~

Brett and Anthony strolled out of the dining room onto the porch. They noticed the commotion at the far end of the walkway to their left and stood watching for a moment. As they watched and listened, Chris came around the corner and crashed into the two men. "I'm so sorry!" he exclaimed, "Are you okay?"

Brushing mud off themselves both men replied that they were. Noting the debris and mud splattered on Chris's clothing, hands and face they asked him what was wrong. He simply shook his head and, replied, "I just slipped on the wet grass."

Brett looked at Anthony, fear obvious in his blue eyes. "What do you think happened?" Anthony shrugged and wrapped an arm around Brett's waist. "Don't know, but we need to clean up! Meet you back here in twenty?"

Brett smiled and nodded, but he was feeling uneasy and feared there was something more than what had been told to them.

By the time Chris got back to the dining room, Dave had taken Maria to the office and had her somewhat calmer although still quite shaken up. Dave looked up and gasped as he saw how disheveled Chris was, "Oh my God! Are you okay?"

He nodded and leaned on the desk before falling into the nearest chair. Seeing her boss in such a state, Maria began sobbing again. Dave quieted her down then turned to Chris. "What happened?" he asked in hushed tones.

Between heavy, labored breaths, Chris uttered two shaky words, "It's Craig."

Dave didn't understand Chris's implication. "What about Craig? Did he finally make it in?"

Chris shook his head, "No. He never left."

"Chris, what the hell are you talking about?"

Softly, Chris told him, "Craig's dead."

The room became as still and quiet as the morgue Craig's body would soon be in. Dave fell into the chair behind the desk, his mouth agape, eyes wide. "No," he repeated over and over. "No, it can't be. This can't be happening!" His hands trembled and he felt bile rise in his throat.

He looked over at Maria; she was nodding her head, her eyes red and puffy, but otherwise calming down. Dave picked up the phone and dialed 9-1-1. After giving the requested information he turned his attention to his employee. "Maria, you can go home if you want to. You've been through enough for one day."

The young woman shook her head. "No, Mr. Dave, I'll stay. Work, it will take my mind away from what I saw."

Dave smiled wanly. "Thank you. Take all the time you need before starting work. I need to take Chris to clean up."

Maria nodded and managed a trembling smile as her bosses left her alone in the silent room.

The small crowd outside on the patio had dispersed as Dave led Chris to their private apartment to clean up. Dave's mind reeled with the ramifications of the events of the early morning, not knowing what to say, if anything, to their guests.

While Chris cleaned up Dave cleared the soiled clothing, not wanting Chris to see them. He stood at the bathroom door for a moment, listening for the shower, then hearing it run he turned to the bed and threw himself on the comforter, allowing himself a moment to absorb and react to what had just transpired. "Craig is dead," he kept repeating, trying to force understanding of that horrific fact. He didn't cry, he was numb and that bothered him. He had known Craig from before they'd purchased Raven Hall. He'd admired the young man for his zest for life and his ability to see the bright side of almost every situation. "I'll never see him again!" he muttered aloud and sat up on the edge of the bed. Without realizing it, tears had started flowing down his cheeks. He wiped them away with the back of his hand just as Chris emerged from the bathroom. He managed a sad smile. "Feel a bit better?"

Chris shrugged. "A little."

Dave stood and embraced him. "You get dressed, I'm going to go out and wait for the police. I want to direct them onto Sugan Street. We don't need squad cars with their sirens blaring pulling into our parking lot."

He turned at the door and without a word being said the two men exchanged a worried look; their peace and quiet had been violated.

It wasn't long before the sound of distant sirens grew closer and the flashing blue and red lights crested over the rise east of the resort. Dave had gone to the intersection and when the black and white approached, waved his arms to signal the approaching squad car. He approached the driver's door and asked the officer to pull around the corner on Sugan Street. "I'd rather not alarm our guests," he explained.

As the officer swung onto Sugan Street, Dave made his way through the wooded lot, meeting the officer at his squad car and began to lead him to the bloodied remains of not only an employee but a friend. It wasn't long before he and the officer saw the pooled blood and then the sprawled feet. Dave stopped short; he could go no farther and felt his head begin to swim. "You okay?" the officer asked.

Dave nodded, "I'm okay, but I don't think I can go any farther." With that he pointed. The officer caught sight of the crimson puddle and cautiously sidestepped it, not wanting to disturb any possible evidence. As he examined and began cordoning off the area with yellow crime scene tape, Dr. Driscoll arrived. He smiled and nodded briefly to Dave then approached the officer, "Hey, Don!"

"Good morning, Doc. Pretty gruesome sight, huh?"

"You can say that again." Dr. Driscoll scanned the area and began taking photos of the scene. After photographing the body and the immediate area he started backtracking. "Did you notice any footprints?"

Officer Compton shook his head. "There are too many to distinguish any specific ones. This is a well-used path."

Dr. Driscoll moved back into the area near the body. "Here." He photographed a set of prints right next to the body. "These can't be the victim's, he's wearing dress shoes, these are made by either sneakers or work boots." He placed his foot next to the deep imprint. "A bit larger than mine, probably a size 10 ½ or 11."

As the investigation of the crime scene continued, the day grew warm and more humid. Dave found it difficult to breathe and was beginning to perspire. He'd dared to glance over to the cordoned off area a few times, but each time he did, he began to shake, and although he was perspiring heavily, he was shivering uncontrollably. "Officer, if you don't need me any longer."

Noticing the sheen of sweat on his face and the way he was shaking, Officer Compton cut him off. "No, go ahead back. I'll be up to the office to speak to you as soon as we've wrapped things up here. Where can I find you?"

"Office, far end of the resort."

Dave gratefully left the gruesome scene to the two professionals. Dr. Driscoll looked up from his work and watched Dave depart.

~ ~ ~

Brett tossed the soiled shorts and T-shirt on the chair near the window and went into the bathroom to wash the mud off his arms and legs. Only then did he notice that the mud had a reddish tint to it. "Huh, that's odd." He rubbed the dark soil between his fingers. Figuring it was Pennsylvania clay he washed it off.

Feeling refreshed now that he'd cleaned up and put on fresh clothing, Brett's thoughts returned to spending the day and hopefully the night with Anthony. He smiled as he left his room and mounted the stairs to the main walkway of the resort. Anthony was coming down the path towards his room; Brett stopped and admired the sight and his smile broadened. Unlike so many gay men, Anthony was wearing board shorts and they fit him perfectly. Brett despised the garish speedos that seemed to dominate gay culture. He himself preferred to leave a little to the imagination; he didn't need to see every bulge and crevice in a man's body. "Nice," he muttered as Anthony neared. Anthony's body was lean and toned, and being all Italian, his skin was naturally browned. His hair was short and brushed straight back from his forehead. As he approached, Brett studied his walk; there was a bit of a swagger, probably from growing up in Brooklyn. He seemed in control of his body as well as the environment around him. "Damn!"

"I was just coming to get you."

"Well, you got me! Let's go. You look great by the way."

"Yeah? So do you. I like those shorts, and the way you fill them out!"

~ ~ ~

A sharp rap on the office door startled the still shaken owners. Chris sat behind the desk, staring at the blotter, and Dave couldn't wipe the image of Craig's splayed feet and the blood from his mind. "It's open," Dave managed.

Officer Compton stepped in from the bright sunlight to the dimness of the office. "Am I disturbing something?"

Dave stood and walked toward him, "Not at all, Officer. Chris is still shook up and I'm not doing much better. Please," he motioned to a chair. Officer Compton settled into the tufted leather arm chair and Dave leaned on the corner of the desk, near Chris. "What did you determine so far?"

Compton shook his head, "Not much I'm afraid. I came in to get some basic information about the deceased."

"Certainly. What is it you need?"

"The basics, name, age, address, next of kin."

"I have that right here on the computer. It'll just take me a few moments to locate it."

Officer Compton smiled and nodded. As Dave booted up the desktop he looked around at the room, noting the dark paneled wood. "Nice room. Who decorated it?"

Focused on the screen Dave replied, "It was like this when we purchased the place. I like it, Chris thinks it's too dark and depressing. Ah, here it is. I can print it out if you'd like."

"That would be great. Thanks." While they waited for the print out, Officer Compton continued his questioning. "I need to ask some rather personal questions about Craig."

"Such as?"

"Did he have a lover?"

"No. He's been single for some time now. He and Don broke up about a year or so ago."

"Is he still around?"

Dave shook his head, "He moved to Arizona right after the break up."

"How about his friends? Did he live alone or have a roommate?"

"He had to share an apartment, he couldn't swing it on his own, especially after Don left."

"Do you have the roommate's name?"

"It's . . . ah, crap, I can't remember. Can I get it to you later?"

"Sure. One more thing and I apologize in advance for this question. Was he promiscuous?"

With that, Chris's head snapped up, "What?"

"Sorry, but it's important."

Chris sighed then laughed, shaking his head. "Craig could be, shall we say, 'popular'."

Compton grinned, "Nicely put. Only a few more things, I need to know what he did last night, before. . ."

Dave, seeing the look on Chris's face, answered. "Well, he worked last night."

"Doing what?"

"He waited tables."

"Did you happen to notice if he was being particularly attentive or friendly with any of the guests?"

Dave sighed. "God, we were so busy I don't know but I don't see how he could have been. It was a madhouse and he would have had enough to do to serve the guests, let alone flirt with any of them."

Compton nodded. "What time did he finish work?"

"About midnight, I believe."

"And after that? Did he give any indication about what he was going to do?"

Dave chuckled, "He said he was too wound up to sleep and wanted to play."

"Excuse me? Play?"

Chris stood and walked towards the window. "He was going to have a few drinks and 'socialize', if anything happened all the better."

"Oh, I see. Did either of you see him with anyone?"

Both men shook their heads, "I was in the office," Chris answered, "and Dave had retired for the evening."

Closing his notebook, Officer Compton stood and smiled. He headed towards the door. "Oh," he said, "Dr. Driscoll will be here shortly to give you his findings. If either of you think of anything else or if someone comes to you with information please get in touch with me immediately." Chris stopped him before he could leave, "Officer, do you at least have a motive? Why would someone do such a thing?"

The hot blond cop shook his head, "I don't know. I can tell you that it wasn't robbery. He still had his wallet, keys and cash on him. Other than that I couldn't say." With that he stepped into the heat of the day. He scanned the grounds, noting the secluded surroundings and the number of guests at the pool, on the patio and in the bar, wondering if one of them was the killer. As it stood now, however, they were all suspects.

~ ~ ~

SATURDAY AFTERNOON
New Hope, Pennsylvania

Brett and Anthony lounged by the pool for a few hours, enjoying the sun, the water and each other. Just after noon, Brett sat up, "Want to get a bite to eat?"

Anthony thought for a moment, "Nah, not hungry. You?"

"I'm just tired of sitting here. I want to do something."

"How about going into town and do some shopping?"

Brett nodded, "Sounds good. Let's do that."

They pulled on their sneakers and T-shirts and headed towards the parking lot. Anthony said he'd drive; a small gesture that Brett interpreted as wanting to be in control. *That was the way Alan was!*, he thought as he slid into the passenger's seat.

The town was packed and they found it difficult to navigate the narrow sidewalks without bumping into someone coming the opposite way. There were many unique shops along the main street but instead of going in they simply window shopped, pointing out different and sometimes one-of-a-kind items on display in the windows. The one shop Brett insisted on going into was the candy shop, the aroma of chocolate and other sweets proving to be too much for him to resist. After Brett fulfilled his need for sugar, they walked slowly back down the main street stopping only at the bridge over a scenic waterfall to admire the serenity of the view, a momentary respite from the crowded and noisy street.

Finally around two, Brett commented that he was now hungry. They opted to sit at the bar at Havana's and have a drink with their late lunch. Finding himself relaxed by the warm air and the company Brett dared to ask Anthony some personal questions. "Can I ask you something?" he started just after they ordered.

"Sure, I have no secrets."

"Well, I was just wondering if you see anything between us after this weekend. I mean is this just a holiday fling for you, or are you looking for something real?"

Anthony grinned the crooked grin Brett had come to find very attractive. "Brett, I don't do flings, as you put it. I haven't had a relationship for a long time, didn't want one, but I think I'm ready to try again."

"Try? I'm an experiment?"

Anthony sat up and took Brett's hands in his, "No, no that's not what I mean. I'm strong enough to want to be with someone special. One day I'll tell you what happened to make me so guarded, but for now suffice to say it was bad and it took me a long time to recover."

"Sorry, I shouldn't have jumped to that conclusion."

Anthony smiled and winked at him.

They spent the rest of the afternoon talking about themselves and the various experiences that brought them to the point in their lives that they now found themselves in. A few hours later they made their way to Anthony's Toyota and back to Raven Hall. The main lots being full, they parked behind the strip mall across from the resort.

As they walked across West Bridge Street, Brett commented. "It's quiet, isn't it?"

Anthony shrugged. "The calm before the storm."

Brett shook his head. "No, there's something wrong." He spied Chris and Dave talking to someone in hushed tones; they stopped their conversation abruptly as they approached. He stopped short and wrapped his arms about himself. Anthony noticed and took him by the shoulder past the three men, who smiled as they passed, and into the bar. "You need a drink!"

~ ~ ~

The detective assigned to the case spent the majority of the late morning and afternoon interviewing Chris and Dave. He took copious notes and had the crime scene photographer take many more pictures. "Be sure to document anything you think might be relevant," Detective Scott directed him. He then turned his attention to Officer Compton, the first responder. "And be sure to keep everyone out of that area! We don't want the scene contaminated, at least any more than it already might be." After the photographer and officer left, Detective Scott turned his attention back to the two owners.

"Okay," he started as he pondered where to go next in this perplexing investigation. "According to you," he pointed to Chris, "you were alerted to the remains by one Maria Alvarez."

Chris nodded. "She's on our housekeeping staff."

"If she's here I'd like to speak to her."

Dave stood. "I'll get her."

Detective Scott paced the walkway that fronted the rooms. "Nice place. You guys did a great job at redoing it. Must have cost a fortune."

Chris chuckled. "Thanks, and yes, it cost a rather sizable fortune."

"How did you two manage to afford doing all this?"

"Well, Detective," Chris began, his arms folded defensively in front of him. "We have some sizable loans to repay and we both used most of our personal savings." He shot the older man a distasteful look.

Detective Scott felt the anger in Chris's stare. "Sorry, I didn't mean to pry."

Chris waved his hand, "That's okay. I guess I'm on edge what with all this happening on our so-called grand opening. We worked almost a year getting this place ready. We were so happy that we were booked and would be okay considering the amount of capital that went into this place. And now!"

Their conversation was interrupted as Dave and Maria approached, "Is there somewhere we can talk in private?" the detective asked.

Dave led them to the office at the end of the walkway. "There, the office is at the foot of the stairs." He stood aside. "If you won't be needing us any longer we need to attend to our guests."

Detective Scott shook his head. "If one of you would stay."

Chris nodded and led the way.

The interview with Maria was brief; she only saw the body a few hours ago and the time of death was long before that. After she left Detective Scott decided to survey the resort. He never understood the gay life style, but having lived in Bucks County all his life and having served on the New Hope Police Force for almost 18 years now, he knew many personally and had acquiesced to their presence, almost. He harbored no real prejudice towards gay men, but now, being here and seeing the way some of them carried on at the pool, how they swished around, how they called each other "Mary," or "she," he found some of his earlier bigotry returning. "This isn't going to be easy," he muttered as he descended the stairs and searched out Officer Compton. Spotting him near the far end of the walkway, he put his head down and forged ahead.

Officer Compton spotted the detective and started approaching him. "Detective," he began, but was stopped by his superior who barked, "Anything?"

Compton shook his head, "Not much. No one saw or heard a thing. A few of the guys saw the victim with a man but none recognized him. Most of the men here aren't local, so getting an ID is next to impossible."

"That's what I was afraid of. What else do you have?"

Compton went through his notes, apprising the detective of the important details necessary for him to at least start his investigation; all the while Detective Scott was scanning the crowd of men, searching each face, wondering if one of them could be the murderer. After Compton finished his report, Detective Scott nodded and started walking off towards the crime scene. He paused part way down the staircase ordering, "Make sure you get a complete list of every guest here. We need to speak to every one of them."

Compton nodded and went off in search of the owners.

~ ~ ~

Anthony and Brett sat together at a small table in the Oak Room Piano Bar, at the back of the resort. This room, Anthony thought, would do a great deal to relax Brett. Its rich dark wood paneling and coffered ceiling lent an air of quiet calmness to the large room. At first Anthony tried to engage Brett in conversation, but soon realized that Brett wasn't responding. "Brett? Hello! If you aren't going to talk to me then I might as well leave you here alone."

Brett looked over at him, "What?"

"Well, you can talk!" He smiled and took Brett's face in his hands. "Don't make me worry about you."

Brett smiled slightly, "I'm sorry. I just can't shake this feeling that there's something wrong here. It's like I've suddenly been thrust into someone's nightmare."

Anthony feigned hurt at that comment. "You think I'm a nightmare?"

Brett laughed, "No, not you. That!" Whatever is going on out there."

Anthony's eyes followed Brett's stare. "There's nothing going on out there." He stated sternly. "You need to go back to your room and relax."

Brett stood, "Yeah I think I will." He rose quickly and started walking towards the exit then turned back. "Aren't you coming?"

Anthony was at his side instantly.

As they walked towards his room, Anthony couldn't help worrying about Brett's state of mind. "Look, you don't even know what happened. Don't make it something more than it is! Okay?"

As they neared the corner and turned down the path that led to Brett's room the reality of the matter became quite evident; a body was being lifted into the back of the coroner's van. Brett froze and couldn't take his eyes off the macabre scene. Anthony focused his attention to where his companion was staring. "Holy shit!" was all he could say.

As they stared, it became evident that Brett's fears were realized. As much as he wanted to run from the scene, to erase it from his mind's eye Brett found his feet cemented to the walkway.

He didn't speak, didn't breathe; he simply stared. Anthony took his arm and started to pull him back away from the grizzly sight. Brett shook, startled by Anthony's touch then turned and started down the stairs to his room. From the crime scene a man had taken note of them.

~ ~ ~

Dave and Chris spent most of the remainder of the afternoon with various members of the New Hope P.D. They had answered the same questions for what seemed to be a hundred times, each time responding the same way. Maria had been interrogated in a similar manner. After hours of questioning, she left for the day, exhausted more from the mental anguish than the physical labor. By 5 P.M. Dave and Chris were finally alone in their office. The silence was deafening; the only sound was that of the Regulator clock on the back wall. "You hungry?" Dave asked.

Chris shook his head.

"You should try to eat something. You haven't had a bite of food since early this morning."

"I can't eat, and I doubt I'll be able to sleep for a long, long time." He looked up at his life partner, tears evident in his eyes.

Dave came to him and took him in an embrace. "You'll be all right," he repeated as he held Chris. "We'll be all right, and so will Raven Hall," he added strongly.

The tragic events of the morning caused Dave to realize that he would have to be in control more than ever. Where he would find the bravado to rise to the situation, he didn't know, all he did know was that Chris needed his strength and he would muster up as much as he could.

Chris buried his head in Dave's chest and sobbed quietly, drawing comfort from him. Shortly he found his eyes closing and his body giving in to the rigors of the emotional stress that was exhausting him. Sensing his body slacken; Dave helped him to the sofa and eased him down onto the tufted leather. Chris didn't open his eyes or speak; he just let himself be eased into a deep slumber.

Dave sat on the edge of the sofa, gently stroking Chris's hair. He smiled down at him as Chris's features softened in sleep. Carefully, Dave stood and retrieved an old throw from the back of the nearby arm chair and draped it over Chris. Planting a brief kiss on his forehead, Dave left his lover to rest.

~ ~ ~

Brett sat on the edge of the bed motionless. Seeing the black body bag being loaded into the back of the coroner's van had a profound effect on him. He remembered as a child coming home to see a similar scenario outside his own home. He ran into the house terrified about what he might see, crying uncontrollably, convinced that either his mother or father had died. To his relief, however the van was there because their next elderly door neighbor had passed away. Still, the sight of the black van and the body bag renewed the terror of that night so long ago.

Anthony didn't know what to do to comfort him. He only knew that he had to be there, had to let Brett know that he cared even though he didn't understand his reaction to the events of the holiday morning. Finally, he came to Brett and sat next to him, "Listen," he said; his voice soft and comforting, "We don't know what happened to whoever it was they put into that van. I mean he or she could have been drunk and fallen and hit their head or something. Don't let your imagination run wild." He took Brett's hands in his, "My God! Your hands are ice cold!"

Brett looked up into Anthony's deep brown eyes, "Well then, warm them up for me."

Anthony didn't know if he was being serious or seductive; he simply sat next to him holding both his hands between his. Shortly, Brett leaned over and rested his head on Anthony's shoulder. They sat there silently for a while the only sounds were the muffled voices of the other guests wafting in from outside.

It was Anthony who began to lie down on the soft bed, pulling Brett down with him. They lie side by side, enjoying the warmth and firmness of each other's bodies. Brett leaned up on one elbow and kissed Anthony deeply, "Thank you."

"For what?"

"A lot of guys would have turned and walked away earlier today when I started freaking out about what we just saw, but you stayed. That tells me a lot about you."

Anthony sat up and smiled. "Oh yeah? Like what?"

"Well, for one thing that you're not just looking to have sex, that you're a caring person and that you're who and what you say you are; there's no pretense to you."

Anthony nodded, "Okay, I'll agree to that. I am a good catch! But, my good man, I don't know who caught whom yesterday."

Brett thought for a moment, "Hmm, let's just say it was a mutual catch, shall we."

With that he kissed Anthony again, this time deeper, longer and more passionately.

~ ~ ~

The night had become chilled by the time the sun set. Dr. Driscoll wrapped up his report. Noting the time and hoping that his wife would be holding dinner for him, he slid the body into the cooler and headed home. Once there he sat in the car and prepared himself for what he feared he would find. Exhaling deeply he pressed the visor mounted remote control that raised the garage door and pulled the Mercedes into the garage. Hoping he would find a sober wife and a hot dinner he entered the home through the steel door into the kitchen. The room was empty and quiet, as was the rest of the house. There were some lights on, those that operated on a timer, other than that there was only darkness and silence. He knew, without even thinking about it, that she would be in bed, passed out, a bottle of wine on the night stand. His stomach knotted as he mounted the carpeted staircase and entered the master suite. As he suspected, she was splayed across the bed still fully dressed and there, on the night stand was the usual bottle of wine, this time a merlot. He shook his head and stripped out of his suit. His habit was to shower not only in the morning, but upon returning home, wanting to wash the smell of death from his skin. He stayed in the large walk-in shower for a long time, letting the hot water and soap not only wash away the stench of death, but the anguish of their rapidly failing marriage.

He dressed in comfortable jeans, sweatshirt and sneakers and headed back to the kitchen, leaving Adriana sleeping atop the king size bed. He searched the kitchen for something to prepare for dinner but found the pickings slim. Sighing, he snatched his keys from the counter and headed back out, something he did not want to do.

~ ~ ~

The room grew warm as Brett and Anthony's lovemaking grew more passionate. Slowly they removed each other's shirts then the shorts they were wearing were slid down a bit. Hot hands groped firm thighs, butts and finally, as the trunks were stepped out of, engorged shafts. Brett moaned deeply, he couldn't remember the last time he'd been willing to give himself so freely to a man who was in reality still a stranger. His head spun as Anthony's lips, tongue and teeth kissed licked and nibbled his neck, nipples and stomach. Sweat beaded and trickled down his twitching body and his face flushed with passion. Finally their naked bodies intertwined, Anthony's trembling hands put on the condom and their bodies became one. Brett grunted and moaned in ecstasy as he was entered; his eyes never closing, their stare locked onto Anthony's face. As their bodies moved in rhythmically, their breathing became more and more erratic until, with one final thrust Anthony moaned, his climax imminent, Brett sensed this and knew his own release was near. Moments later their sweat soaked-bodies heaved in the intensity of the release.

They lie intertwined for long moments, neither wanting to break the intimate contact. Finally Anthony rolled onto his back and snuggled next to Brett. He was instantly wrapped in Brett's still shaking arms; neither one spoke. Shortly they drifted into a comforting sleep.

~ ~ ~

SATURDAY EVENING
New Hope, Pennsylvania

The evening was inky dark, moonless. The only light came from the street lamp on the corner. Mike pulled into the lot behind the strip mall and sat silently, contemplating what he was about to do, but feared doing. His desires were at the breaking point and the longer he sat alone in the dark lot the more strained they became. He closed his eyes and took deep, cleansing breaths, trying desperately to calm himself. Finally after several moments he felt calm enough to exit the car and approach Raven Hall; he only hoped the young man he'd seen earlier in the day would be alone. He smiled at that thought and picked up his pace, he wanted to get there so he could waylay the fair-haired man he'd spied earlier, before anyone else could.

Both the main bar and the back Oak Room Piano Bar were already crowded. He stood at the head of the short staircase separating the two rooms scanning for the fair-haired one; he was nowhere to be seen. He elbowed his way through the men at the main bar and got a beer.

He positioned himself near the far wall, giving him the advantage of being able to see both rooms simultaneously. As the rooms grew more and more crowded, he became more at ease. This many men would give him the anonymity he needed. The cool, slightly bitter taste of the beer added to his comfort level and he found himself smiling; his mind filling with erotic thoughts of the man he desired.

A sudden sobering thought pierced through his newly found calm: what if he was at the patio bar or the cabana bar? He gulped the rest of the beer and headed out, his head pivoting back and forth searching for his quarry; nothing. He found a new perch half way between the porch and patio and settled in for the long haul. *He has to come here soon,* he thought as he relaxed and watched the various groups of men, their interactions stirring his desires. His breathing became heavy as his attention focused on one couple making out in the corner of the patio bar. No one else seemed to notice that their make out-session was growing more and more passionate, with hands grasping and squeezing, tongues licking, lips sucking. Soon they were visibly aroused and after a few words were spoken between, left to continue in private. He almost followed them to watch, but opted not to. The fair one was sure to come soon, then he would have what he really wanted.

~ ~ ~

In room 12, down and away from the noise and crowds, Brett and Anthony lie together. Their love-making had ended, but their need for intimacy still lingered. Neither had stirred, neither wanted to. It was dark before either of them spoke; "You hungry?" Anthony asked.

"A little. You?"

"I could go for something."

They unwound from each other and dressed. "I hope we're not too late to get something to eat."

"What time is it anyway?"

Brett picked up his watch, "Almost 9." He looked up at Anthony, and laughed. "I had no idea it was that late, did you?"

"Not at all. Come on, let's go."

They left the room hand in hand, feeling the warmth and closeness that only making love could bring about.

~ ~ ~

Mike barely moved, didn't speak, he simply waited. He'd consumed several beers by this time and they were having the desired numbing effect on him. He smiled at single men as they passed him, winking at a few, but still determined to wait the arrival of his quarry. His mind wandered back to the couple he watched earlier, they had not returned and he knew that they were in bed, naked, doing to each other what he needed to do to the fair one. He became aroused as he pictured the two shaved headed men together, using each other - licking, biting, pinching and even penetrating each other. His hands shook and he realized he would have to fulfill his urges soon, fair one or not. The Coors Lights had taken their toll on him too. He staggered slightly to the men's room and joined the line that had formed and waited his turn. He didn't see Brett and Anthony enter the dining room.

Another hour, and a few more beers later, he began not caring so much as to who it would be, but that it would happen. Desire had grown into pure raging need and he began hunting for a single man who appeared to be alone and in need. He stopped drinking and slowly stalked the main and the patio bars, finally finding a suitable substitute near the main entrance. He smiled and approached.

After a brief conversation he had the man. As they crossed West Bridge Street towards his car he became aroused, thinking that his needs would soon be met. The young man was equally aroused and this made him smile. His breathing increased and his heart rate rose; although not who he really wanted, he thought, this man would do nicely.

Thinking they were heading to his place, the young man slid into the passenger's seat, "Nice," he commented as he felt the supple leather interior. "We going to your place?"

The killer shook his head, "No."

"Okay, we can head out to my apartment; it's only a few blocks from here."

Again he shook his head. "Here."

The young man was taken aback by the comment, but at the same time aroused and intrigued at the thought of having sex in the open. He shrugged and stated, "Okay, let's get started."

With the steering wheel tilted upright and the seats of the luxury sedan reclined, the windows soon became steamed up as their making out intensified. Finally they managed to wriggle out of their shirts and pants, their bodies already slick with sweat. He leaned back to take a good look at the young man, stroking his shaft as he did. The man watched and stroked himself in response. Their eyes locked as they continued their mutual masturbation. Within minutes he was moaning loudly and his right hand moved furiously on his erection and his left hand pinched his firm nipples hard. His companion watched; mouth open and dry as he too felt his climax near. His head lolled back and his eyes closed as he erupted. He moaned and grunted as his climax subsided. His eyes still shut he heard the moans of immanent climax from his trick. He opened his eyes to watch as the man completed the act.

Both men were breathing heavily as their bodies calmed and their heart rates returned to normal. The young man smiled. "Man that was great!" he enthused, "I needed that." He pulled up his jeans and zippered them. "We should do this again." He buckled his belt. "You live around here?" He looked up at his partner and saw he was sitting there, his hand still on his rapidly diminishing erection, pants still at his ankles, staring at him. "Hey, you okay?"

Mike nodded. "Thanks. I have to go."

Realizing he was being dismissed, the young man opened the door and got out. He took a few steps on the gravel a bit disappointed at the brush off. Then he heard, "Hey buddy." He turned, thinking his sex partner had a change of heart, and saw the glint off the blade as it struck his throat.

Mike finished buckling his belt, staring down at the still heaving form of whoever that was bleeding out onto the pebbled parking lot and grinned. He hoisted the warm corpse by the legs and dragged it to the slight slope at the rear of the lot, near the stream and rolled it down. He watched as its arms and legs flailed about as it tumbled. He then wiped the blade and tossed it into the rapidly running stream, knowing it would be impossible to see under the glinting water. Returning to his car, he exhaled. His urges were satisfied - for now.

~ ~ ~

Brett and Anthony, relaxed and still in euphoria of love making, spent over two hours in the dining room. Their meals had been finished long ago, and the room had emptied, save for the staff and the host who'd seated them together on Friday evening. He smiled broadly when he'd seen them enter earlier hand-in-hand. "Ah, spring time and love is in the air!" he cooed. He approached the table and said, "Stay as long as you like!"

Alone in the large room, they sipped snifters of Grand Marnier talking in hushed tones about themselves. Each found it easy to relate past events in their lives without fear of judgment, over reaction or the need to give hindsight advice.

Anthony leaned back sideways in his chair, running his index finger around the rim of the crystal glass. Staring down at the warm, orange liquor, he started, "You know, you're something else."

"What do you mean?"

Anthony leaned forward, crossing his bronzed arms in front of him on the linen tablecloth. "I don't remember the last time I felt so comfortable being with someone. You've broken through most of my defenses."

Brett raised his eyebrows, "Most!"

Anthony's voice was barely a hair above a whisper, "I'd promised myself I would never do certain things again, but you," he pointed into Brett's candlelit face, "you've made me break three of those promises."

"And they are, or were?"

Anthony clicked them off on his fingers. "First, don't date guys from Jersey!

Brett rolled his eyes at that.

"Second, don't sleep with anyone until at least a month after dating him."

"And third?"

Anthony swallowed hard, his deep chestnut eyes glistening. "Never," he was whispering now, "Never fall in love."

Brett's lip began quivering and he welled up, immediately wiping the tears from his eyes. Anthony laughed at Brett's response as he too used the cloth napkin to wipe his own eyes.

Unbeknownst to either man, the entire dining room staff had stopped work and was straining to hear their conversation. The host, Joseph, better known to locals as "Mother" for his extensive drag wardrobe and shows, let out a scream, barely hearing those three little words. He and the rest of the staff made a hasty albeit noisy giggling retreat into the kitchen.

The moment broken, Anthony and Brett lapsed into fits of laughter. "Oh my God!" Brett said when he finally regained his composure. "That scared the hell out of me."

Still laughing, Anthony replied, "Me too. Did you know they were there?"

"No! I was too wrapped up in you and what you were saying to even know there was anyone anywhere."

Anthony reached across the table and took Brett's hands in his, "Mmm, warm."

"Anthony? Stay with me tonight."

Anthony nodded.

CHAPTER IV

EARLY SUNDAY MORNING, May 27th
New Hope, Pennsylvania

Medical Examiner Driscoll arrived early Sunday morning to begin the arduous task of looking for forensic evidence on the body of Craig Jamison. He'd sent a text to his assistant, Emily Hargrove, and she arrived shortly before 7 A.M. "What do we have, Doc?" she asked as she began unzipping the black poly body bag. But before the doctor could respond he heard her gasp, "Holy shit!"

He chuckled as he prepared the scalpel to start work. "Now you know."

She turned and held her gloved hands to her face, "Oh my God! I've never seen anything like that!"

Dr. Driscoll finished removing the body while Emily took a few moments to regain her composure. Once calmed she came to his side. "I assume we're not performing an autopsy."

"Uh huh," he muttered in response as he began probing Craig's gashed throat. "We need to look for any possible evidence; hair, other than the victim's, possible skin under the nails which would indicate a struggle, maybe even semen."

Emily shot him a confused look. "He was murdered near Raven Hall", he stated.

She nodded in understanding, then looked into the pale, bluish face of what had once been Craig Jamison. "Handsome guy."

Dr. Driscoll glanced up. "Yes, he was."

"Who would do such a thing?" "You'll see much worse than this in your career," he replied absently as he began cutting away Craig's muddied and blood-soaked clothing. "Grab me a paper bag for these things."

For the next hour or so the two worked in silence searching for any evidence that could help the police direct their investigation. By 9 A.M. they had completed all they could. "Well," sighed Dr. Driscoll, "That's all we can do for now." He snapped off the latex gloves and plastic gown, "You go on home, Em. I'll write up the report."

She nodded gladly and stripped off her own gown and gloves, tossing them into the hazards container as she left.

Alone in the morgue, Dr. Driscoll took another look into Craig's cold face.

~ ~ ~

Detective Scott sat with the stained, cracked coffee mug in his raised right hand. He'd been sitting stoically for several minutes, scanning over the preliminary report of the M.E. Finally he put the cold coffee down and pushed the faxed sheets away.

"Damn it!" he exclaimed. "Nothing. Not a God blessed friggin' solid bit of evidence!"

He rubbed his bleary eyes and began pacing his cramped office. Although the room itself was fairly sizable, the clutter of file cabinets, chairs, a worn sofa and electronic equipment closed it in around him.

He shook his head as he looked around, *I should be on that Hoarders program!*

He snatched up the *World's Greatest Dad* mug and went out into the main office to dump the cold coffee and replace it with fresh brew. Though it was Sunday, a full staff was on duty. Memorial Day weekend, the unofficial kickoff of the summer season, brought with it its share of drunken brawls and family disputes and the small force had to be prepared. He noticed that the large fluorescently lit room was quiet, eerily so, and it unnerved him. The entire New Hope P.D. of fewer than one hundred officers had been alerted to the murder last Friday and was on edge. Murder was a rare occurrence in such a small, laid back burg.

Filling his cup with the rapidly overheating brew, he returned to his office, closing the door behind him. He sat silently for a moment, sipping a bit of the bitter coffee, grimaced and put it aside. "It has to be done," he stated aloud. He grabbed his keys and was out of the door in a flash.

CHAPTER V

LATE SUNDAY MORNING, May 27th
New Hope, Pennsylvania

Chris and Dave were taken aback by the Sunday morning visit of the detective. Most of the guests were still asleep, or otherwise engaged in their rooms, while a few were enjoying a cup of coffee on the patio, using the caffeine to eradicate the cerebral cobwebs spun by the previous night's drinking.

Detective Scott walked slowly past several men, studying their faces as well as their manner of behavior. Something suddenly registered in his somewhat bigoted mind, *these guys look normal.* That was a compliment in his twisted perspective. He had for so long stereotyped gay men that this revelation unnerved him and made him start to rethink his long held opinion of gay people in general. He shrugged and continued on towards the office, hoping that at least one of the owners would be there.

"Who's the suit?" one guest asked of his companion from the night before.

"Don't know, don't care," he responded. "You ready for round two?"

They rose to return to the cool, dark room. "Don't you mean round three?" he grinned and grabbed his companion's tight ass as they walked. "Let's go!"

~ ~ ~

Holding his breath, Scott rapped loudly on the office door.

"Come in." He exhaled. Someone was there.

Chris looked up from the computer screen, surprised at who stood before him. "Detective. Didn't expect to see you again so soon. Is there something more you need from us?" Scott took a seat opposite the ornate desk. "Yes, there is."

Chris sat back into the plush leather desk chair, the hairs on the back of his neck prickling. *This isn't going to be good.*

"I need to lock down the resort."

Chris's brow furrowed. "Lock down? I don't understand."

"No one leaves."

Chris immediately started to protest, but Scott raised his hands, silencing him. "Let me explain."

Scott stood and began pacing as he spoke. "I need to interview each guest and employee. That's the only option I have left if there's any hope of getting this investigation started."

"But," Chris interrupted. "None of the guests and only a few of the staff even know what happened. Doing that could cause a panic. You could ruin our business."

"I've thought about that already. Here's how I intend to proceed."

Detective Scott quickly outlined his plan then sat. Finally, Chris nodded. "Okay. That'll work. When do you want to get started?"

"Now. We can start with members of the staff." As soon as he took out his notepad and pen the detective's cell phone rang.

Chris watched as Scott listened intently, rubbing his brow. "Fuck!" He ended the call and looked over at Chris as he again stood. "I'll be back later." With that he raced out the door.

~ ~ ~

Brett woke slowly to find dappled sunlight filtering in through the curtains. He sensed something was different, then remembered. Anthony lay curled up next to him, snoring slightly. Brett wanted so badly to reach out and touch him, stroke his hair, kiss him, but he also wanted to let him sleep.

As silently as he could, Brett slipped from under the sheets and padded to the bathroom. He leaned on the pedestal sink and stared at his reflection. Despite getting only a few hours sleep he looked refreshed and rested. He laughed aloud, *what the hell are you doing?* Shaking his head, he turned the water in the shower on hot and stepped in.

Leaning on the cool tile wall, he let the steaming water course its way down his chest and back, running in rivulets into every crevice of his firm body. Eyes closed he began washing, massaging the soap across, around and into each spot Anthony had been the night before. A distant smile broke across his face when he felt a third, then a forth hand on him. He leaned back onto Anthony's chest and reached back to grasp his erection. "I thought you were asleep."

"Does that feel asleep?"

Brett turned to face him, their open mouths met passionately. Slick bodies melded as tongues and hands probed, the water cooling as their lovemaking heated up. Anthony took Brett by the shoulders and turned him around, pressing tightly against him, his hips thrusting. Brett pushed back, wanting to complete the act, to unite their bodies once again. Suddenly, he stopped and pulled away. Breathlessly, Anthony asked, "What?"

Brett uttered one word. "Condom."

Anthony pulled the shower curtain back and stepped out. Upon returning the latex protector was already in place. Brett grinned.

"Now," commanded Anthony. "Assume the position."

Brett complied and their two water and sweat-soaked bodies were joined. Once fully connected, neither man moved, neither wanted to. Just being together in this intimate act was, for the moment, satisfying enough.

It was Brett who began to move first. He pushed back and rotated his hips against Anthony who responded by thrusting. At first his movements were slow, then he increased them in intensity as their bodies moved in perfect rhythm. It wasn't long before Anthony was gasping aloud, his climax imminent. Brett, feeling his own orgasm building, pushed back one final time, bringing them both to a trembling climax. Panting heavily, they remained motionless as the water gradually became cold. Brett, his breathing returning to normal, shut the water off and turned to take Anthony in his arms. The kiss they shared was warm and deep, yet soft and loving. Pulling back slightly, he said, "I meant to tell you something last night in the dining room."

Stroking his face with the back of his hand, Anthony asked, "What was it?"

"I love you."

They stood in the empty tub clinging to each other, both with the knowledge that they were now complete.

~ ~ ~

Detective Scott ran as fast as his arthritic legs would allow him across West Bridge Street and behind the strip mall. Breathing hard he stuttered to a stop, taking in the dark scene that confronted him. Yellow crime scene tape cordoned off an area of the parking lot and wooded area beyond. One uniformed officer was gingerly sifting through a green dumpster while another was talking to a rather shaken fifty-something-year-old woman. Scott began walking towards the crime scene, hoping it wasn't a repeat of the Craig Jamison murder.

He paused just outside the cordoned area. Beyond the pebble parking lot lie a gently flowing stream and a shady woods, a tranquil contrast to the flashing squad car lights and their constant crackling radios. Ducking under the yellow plastic, he approached the first responder, Officer Hillard. Hoping against hope he asked, "Is it like the last one?"

Hillard nodded. "'Fraid so, Detective."

"Damn it!" Scott was visibly shaken as he asked, "What do you have so far?"

Hillard flipped the pages of his notepad. "Let's see, male in his late twenties or early thirties, dark hair and eyes. He was fully dressed."

"I.D.?"

Hillard nodded. "His wallet was still on him with his driver's license, credit cards, and cash all there."

Scott ran his fingers through his damp hair. "Method?"

Hillard looked up at the detective. There was no need for a verbal response.

~ ~ ~

Chris had followed Detective Scott to the edge of the parking lot. From there he could see the reflections of the red and blue police lights. He folded his arms across his chest and stared, his body trembling slightly.

Dave's voice echoed down to him, but he remained stationary. The voice grew louder but still he didn't move. Finally a hand grasped him by the shoulder. He flinched and turned.

"Didn't you hear me?" Dave asked. He then noticed Chris's worried face and caught a glimpse of the flashing lights across the street. "Oh no. What happened?"

"Don't know."

Dave took Chris by the arm. "Come on, this probably doesn't concern us."

As they walked back towards the main building, Chris turned to look back.

~ ~ ~

Emily's cell phone buzzed in her purse. She fished it out and checked the display. "Damn it, work! And on a Sunday and a holiday weekend no less."

She wiped bacon grease from her lips and answered. "Hello," was the only word she could get in. Her breakfast grew cold as she listened and jotted down the address. She rose from the kitchen table and slid the remaining bacon and eggs into the garbage disposal and dropped the plate into the stainless steel sink. She ended the call with a brisk, "I'm on my way."

She leaned on the sink for a moment the pushed herself away, grabbed her keys and purse, checked to see that her camera, notepad and pen were there, and slammed out of her condo.

The crime scene we only six or seven miles away, but it took her the better part of forty-five minutes to start-stop in the bumper-to-bumper holiday traffic. As the minutes ticked past she began pounding the steering wheel, and yelling at other drivers to get a move on!

Finally arriving at the crime scene she gathered up her purse and I.D. and crunched her way across the parking lot to the cordoned area. A uniformed officer stopped her, but she flashed her credentials and he moved aside. She ducked under the tape and forced herself to calm down. "Where is he?" she asked the first officer she saw. He pointed with the end of a pencil.

"Ass!" she mumbled. Throughout her young life she'd had a few unpleasant encounters with the law and held onto the resentment of those times like a junkyard dog holds onto a bone.

"Detective Scott?"

He turned. "And you are?"

"Emily Hargrove, Assistant Medical Examiner." She handed him her card.

Scott scanned the area. "Where's Driscoll?"

"He sent me."

The detective looked her up and down. "Oh."

Emily rolled her eyes. "Where's the vic?"

Scott led her to the edge of the drop off to the stream and pointed.

Emily nodded. Her mind flashed back to the remains of the victim from Friday night. *Please no!*

There were several officers scanning the area. "Shit!" Emily groaned. "Hey! You guys could be disturbing potential evidence!" she yelled in a sing-song voice like a mother chiding her unruly children. *They never learn,* she continued to herself as she retrieved her camera and began photographing the scene. Her apprehension escalated as she neared the body. It lie face down in the underbrush near the stream. After snapping several photos with the corpse in that position she asked to have it turned over.

"You sure?" Emily assumed the hands-on-hips posture to which the officers responded by flipping the victim over. Her breakfast began rising up in her throat, but she fought its return. Exhaling loudly, she nodded to the officers and started photographing the body's wounds.

Her mind filled with notes as she snapped away. After several minutes she was satisfied and retrieved small paper bags from her purse. Using masking tape, she affixed a bag to each hand, thus preserving any potential evidence. "Who has his personal effects?"

"I do," an officer replied. "They're in my unit." He stood motionless.

"Well do you think you could get them for me?"

He flinched and left to get the items.

Emily sorted through the items, again taking mental notes. Placing them in another paper bag she looked around. The dappled sunlight glinted off the stream. Birds were flitting in the bright flashes from tree to tree. The recently leafed trees swayed gently in a light breeze. She shook her head at the contradictory scene. As she started back to her car the Coroner's van bumped slowly down the sloping drive to retrieve the body.

Once back at the morgue, Emily helped wheel the remains into the large fluorescently lit exam room. Locking the stainless steel gurney in place she unzipped the heavy black poly bag. The driver stood back, watching.

"Do you think you could give me a hand with this?" she snapped.

"Sorry."

She rolled her eyes as the two of them slid the damp bag down and off the limp form. The driver rolled it up, bloody water dripping onto the tiled floor. Emily glared at him and he quickly grabbed a roll of paper towels and cleaned up the spill. As she began cutting off the shirt and pants from the victim she muttered, "Where the hell do they find these people?"

Once alone in the chilly room, Emily turned on the radio and began her external examination. Flipping through his personal items, she discovered his name was Richard Edmunds. She looked into his ashen face. "Well, hello there, Dick. How you doin?"

Laughing at her own joke she bent forward to examine the wound. Turning on the morgue's recorder she began. "Throat cut across from right to left, about eight or nine centimeters in length. Wind pipe severed as is the right carotid artery." Looking deeper into the wound she continued. "The Onohyoideus muscle is cut between the inferior and superior belly indicating that the blade used was exceedingly sharp and smooth."

She moved down the torso. "No indications of contusions, no lacerations either." Next the paper bags were removed from his hands and the nails were closely examined for signs of a struggle. Debris such as skin or hair could possibly provide DNA and help the police when of if a suspect is taken into custody. "Nothing."

She held up one slightly blue hand. "Nice manicure."

She stepped back and removed her gloves and gown. Recovering the body neatly with a cotton shroud, she unlocked the wheels on the gurney. "Come on, Dickie, time for the deep freeze."

~ ~ ~

Detective Scott returned to Raven Hall and sought out the owners once again. By the time he arrived, the pool area was crowded. Music filled the air as did the voices of the guests. He found Chris and Dave near the dining room overseeing the lunch servers. Scott removed his small notepad from the inside pocket of his suit jacket as he approached. Chris noticed him as he neared and nudged Dave. "Crap, he does not look happy."

Scott nodded and wiped his brow. "Can we talk in private?"

"You stay here," Dave stated to Chris. "I'll speak to the detective in the office."

Chris watched as the two silently walked away.

"Feels good in here," Scott stated as the air conditioning of the office cooled him. "Getting hot outside."

Dave sat erect behind the desk, rubbing his hands together.

"I need to ask if you know one Richard Edmunds."

Dave shook his head. "Name's not familiar." He turned to the computer and pulled up the guest list. His shoulders slumped. "He's a guest."

Scott nodded. "Was."

Dave's entire body grew numb at that one little word. He leaned forward on the desk and buried his face in his hands. Scott sat quietly and waited for him to recover from this latest shock.

His face still covered, Dave asked, "How?"

"Same as Jamison."

"Where?" "Across the street in the rear parking lot."

"When?"

"Sometime last night."

Dave lowered his arms and through watery eyes reiterated the statement Scott had used when he'd first told Chris what he wanted to do. "You were right, Detective. We need to lock down the resort."

Detective Scott nodded then left.

CHAPTER VI

EARLY SUNDAY AFTERNOON, May 27th
New Hope, Pennsylvania

Brett and Anthony lounged near the pool, both men silently sharing the bliss that comes from finding that one person who completes you. The day had become warm as the cool morning breeze faded away.

Anthony dozed, snoring slightly, sweat glistening on his broad, hairless chest while Brett, still energized from their morning lovemaking, sat up and watched the goings-on of the other guests. Some splashed in the pool while others gathered their chairs into groups, obviously gossiping about who hooked up with whom last night, who got shit-faced drunk at the bar and made a complete fool of themselves and who was seen cheating on their lovers.

Brett looked over at Anthony, taking in the sight of the new love in his life from head to toe. He paused mid-body and grinned, still feeling the tingling from having been made love to just a few short hours ago. A loud cheer diverted his attention. Shading his eyes he looked towards the path leading to the pool.

"Holy Mother of God!" He laughed aloud as he shook Anthony awake. "Look at that." He pointed and Anthony, following his finger, sat up. "What the...?" There, coming down the broad staircase was

Raven Hall's resident drag queen, Joseph, aka *Mother*. He, or she, was accompanied by a small entourage of young ladies in waiting. All four of them sauntered through the crowd of admirers, some reaching out to kiss the hand of New Hope's most popular queen. She nodded graciously to each and, as she approached her reserved table and lounge area, greeted the remaining crowd with her signature Queen Elizabeth wave.

As Brett and Anthony were enjoying this slice of living gay history, another small, more serious group approached. Brett gripped Anthony's arm.

"What?"

"Chris and Dave. With that other man. Something's wrong."

Anthony sat up and looked into Brett's crystalline eyes, his brow furrowed.

The music suddenly stopped and every head turned towards the cabana, conversations coming to a stop. For a moment all that could be heard was the bubbling of the pool's filtration system. Then a microphone crackled to life. "Gentlemen, this is Chris Donnely, one of the owners. I need you to listen carefully to the man I'm handing the mic to."

Muffled murmurs rippled through the guests.

"Good morning, or afternoon. I'm Detective Warren Scott of the New Hope Police Department. There's been a rather serious accident involving one of the guests and at this time I'm asking for your cooperation."

The murmuring grew louder.

"I need to speak to each of you briefly to ascertain whether or not you knew, saw, or talked to the man involved in this incident. It won't take long, but it is important."

The murmuring escalated yet again, some men starting to yell out questions, none of which were answered.

Scott continued, "Mr. Donnely will read off several names. When you hear yours please come to the dining room. I'll be there waiting to speak to you. Thank you for your cooperation in this matter."

Thumping was heard as Scott handed the mic back to Chris and exited.

"Okay, guys, the sooner we start the sooner you can get back to sunning or whatever. Can I have Joe Alfano, Ed Brewster and Simon Carter proceed to the dining room, please?" He watched as three men got up, slipped into shorts and a T-shirt and left.

Dave whispered into Chris's ear. "What if someone's not here?"

"The detective has a list of the guests and staff. If anyone isn't here he'll note it, then we'll check their room."

"And what if they're not there? What if...?" "Dave! For Christ sake, how the hell do I know?"

Dave flinched at Chris's angry retort, he'd never seen his lover so angry and it shocked him.

Chris was immediately stunned by his outburst. "I'm so sorry!" he sobbed. "It's just..." Taking him in his arms, Dave stroked his hair. "I know, sweetheart. I know."

CHAPTER VII

LATE SUNDAY AFTERNOON, May 27th
New Hope, Pennsylvania

Chief Medical Examiner Driscoll waited until Emily had completed her report and left the morgue before he came in. Over the past few weeks, whenever they were alone working together, she'd find any excuse to be next to, behind, of in front of him. Even though his marriage was hitting the skids, he was not about to complicate his life even more with an affair. Not to mention that Emily was almost half his age and did have a steady relationship herself.

Turning on the bank of humming fluorescents, he retrieved the body of Richard Edmunds from the cooler. Pulling down the now blood stained shroud he did his own examination of the wound on the victim's neck. Silently, he probed the various throat structures, turning the nearly severed head from side to side. He stood back and let his eyes scan the rest of the ashen corpse. Tossing the sheet back over Edmunds, he wheeled the gurney back into the cooler and proceeded to his office.

After booting up the computer he searched for Emily's *Report of Autopsy* for Richard Edmunds. While scanning the paragraphs he noticed a few statements that didn't quite agree with what he'd just seen moments before. Deleting the phrases in question, he saved the altered report, turned off the computer and made his way out. *She'll learn,* he thought as he locked the door and set the alarm.

He noted the time as he started the Mercedes. *Not yet,* he thought.

~ ~ ~

Brett and Anthony anxiously waited for their names to be called, Brett becoming more and more anxious the longer it took. No one had said a word upon returning from their meeting with Detective Scott, they'd just shake their heads, eyes downcast. This only added to Brett's growing apprehension. Finally, just past three, Brett heard his name. "Come with me," he asked Anthony and the two of them made their way through the subdued crowd.

Detective Scott ran his hands through his thinning hair. He looked up then back and forth between the two thirty-something men who now stood in front of him. "Which one of you is Anders?"

"I am."

"And you are?" he questioned Anthony.

"His boyfriend." Anthony's jaw tightened and he glared down at the detective as he answered.

"Same room?"

"Yeah."

Scott glanced down at the guest list. "There's only one name listed for room 12."

"I'm in that room now as well."

Detective Scott leaned back, his dark eyes fixed on Anthony. "Please wait outside, sir," he ordered. Then, "Please be seated, Mr. Anders."

Brett's eyes shifted nervously between the detective and Anthony as he slowly sat. Scott stayed as he was until Anthony turned to leave.

Before he did, however, he leaned down and kissed Brett. "I'll be right outside if you need me."

After Anthony left, Detective Scott smiled at Brett. "Your boyfriend is rather overprotective."

"He loves me, Detective."

Scott's eyes shifted to the papers in front of him. After verifying Brett's identification and hometown, he got down to the task at hand.

"When did you arrive, Mr. Anders?"

"Friday afternoon."

"Did you come alone?"

"Yes."

A bit surprised by that answer, Scott pressed the issue. "I thought he was your boyfriend? How long have you two been together?"

"We met here Friday evening. Why the personal questions?"

"He..."

"Anthony."

"Excuse me?"

"His name is Anthony."

"Oh. Anthony seems a bit, shall we say, hostile."

"Hostile!" Brett exclaimed. "Why, because he isn't intimidated by you?"

"Now wait just a minute." Scott stood, towering over the seated Brett. "He came in here with a chip on his shoulder and answered my perfectly reasonable questions in an elusive and somewhat angry manner."

Brett could see the detective's point. "Still, I wouldn't say he was hostile."

Scott sat. "I'm sorry, maybe that was a poor choice of words. The events of the past few days have me on edge."

They sat for a moment in silence. Finally, Brett started up the conversation again. "What is it you need to know, Detective?"

Scott smiled. "Did you or Anthony see or hear anything suspicious last night?"

Brett thought for a moment. "I don't think so. We've been spending a lot of time alone together."

"I see."

Brett's next statement stunned the overwrought detective. "Someone else was killed, weren't they?"

Scott's head snapped up. "What did you just say?"

Brett related the details of Friday night to the anxious investigator. "So I've known all along."

"Mr. Anders, please think. Do you recall anything from that night?" Scott moved forward in his chair. "Any unusual sounds, something, *anything* that didn't seem right."

Brett thought. "No, sorry. I guess I was too enthralled with meeting Anthony earlier in the evening to notice anything or anyone else."

"I see." Scott stood. "Thank you, Mr. Anders." The two men shook hands and Brett started to leave.

He hesitated and turned back. "Wait a minute, there was something. I saw a man in the woods. He was near the body, but he was staring up at me."

Scott plopped back down onto the chair, his notepad and pen at the ready. "Describe him."

Brett returned to the chair he'd just vacated, his brow furrowing. "Detective, it was dark." Brett's eyes darted back and forth. "He was thin, dark hair."

"About how old?"

Brett shrugged. "Thirties, maybe."

"Tall, short?"

"Average height."

"Long or short hair?"

"Short."

"Straight or curly?"

"Straight, I think."

"Did you hear him speak?"

"No."

Sitting on the edge of his seat, Detective Scott waited for more information to be forthcoming, but Brett shook his head. "Sorry, that's all I can remember."

"Thank you, Mr. Anders." Scott handed him his card. "Call me if you think of anything else."

Brett nodded then stood to leave.

"One more thing. I'll need your phone number, home and cell."

Confused, Brett asked why he'd need that information.

Scott briefly explained that they might need him to make an identification if and when they arrest a suspect. "Mr. Anders, you might have seen the killer."

Alone at the table, Scott sat stunned at this unexpected turn of events. He didn't hear Chris come in.

"Detective?"

Scott looked up.

"The next guest is here. Shall I send him in?"

Scott shook his head as he gathered up his notepad and pen. "No. I have to see someone else right now." He bolted from the room, leaving Chris and the guest bewildered.

~ ~ ~

Brett found Anthony waiting on the enclosed porch. In front of him were two plates with burgers and steak fries, next to the plates stood two frosted soft drinks. He stood and started to smile as Brett approached, but his handsome features darkened as Brett neared. He came to Brett and took him in his arms, feeling his body tremble slightly. "What's wrong? What happened?"

Brett took in and let out a deep breath, sinking into Anthony's warm embrace. "I need to sit down."

Anthony watched him closely, concern etched on his face. "Brett, tell me what happened. Did he say something out of line?"

"No, no. Nothing like that." He took a long sip of the chilled cola.

"Then what?"

Brett looked into Anthony's worry-ridden eyes and couldn't help but grin. "You won't believe this, but…" He told Anthony the whole story and Detective Scott's reaction. Looking down at the redwood deck, he finished his tale. "I'm still in shock."

Anthony took his hands. "You okay?"

Brett nodded. "Starving!"

For a while they sat in silence, both men satisfying both their physical and emotional needs simply with each other's company and good food. Then from the main building they heard a strained voice calling Brett's name. Anthony was the first to spy Detective Scott nearing. "What the hell does he want now?"

Brett took Anthony's hand and squeezed it a bit hard. Anthony winced.

"I'm sorry, but if I may?" Scott turned to Anthony. "I need to speak to you."

"Me!"

"You were with Mr. Anders Friday night?"

"Yeah, that's when we met."

"You spent the night in his room?"

"That's none of your fucking business!" Anthony stood; his body tense.

Still seated, Brett responded. "No, he did not."

Anthony sat, his eyes still fixed on Scott.

Detective Scott's entire body slackened. "Oh. Then I do apologize for the question."

Brett was curious. "Why did you want to speak with Anthony anyway?"

"Well, I thought that if he spent the night with you then he might have seen something over the fencing that you could have missed, maybe just a few more details that would help." Scott sat with the two men for a while, lost in his own thoughts. Brett and Anthony could tell that he was distraught and that if something didn't happen soon there might be another victim by the time the weekend was over.

Finally Scott stood and left the two men to their now cold burger and fries.

Anthony looked into Brett's downturned eyes. "Hey, where are you?"

"Hmm? Sorry."

"You okay?"

Brett shrugged. "I guess so. I just wish I could have remembered more about Friday night."

He looked at Anthony. "But I was on cloud nine after our first date and didn't see very much at all. Frankly, I'm surprised I recalled as much as I did."

Anthony could see that there was something more than that disturbing him. "What else?"

"I guess I'm a little scared."

"About what the detective said?"

Brett nodded.

Anthony moved closer. "Don't be."

"Wouldn't you be?"

Anthony pulled back, and in his best Brooklyn accent commented. "Yo, I ain't scart of nutin!"

Brett laughed. "But if you were me, wouldn't you be just a little frightened? I mean what if they do catch someone and I have to identify him?"

"Then you do just that."

Brett's head snapped back and down. "I don't know if I could."

"Brett, I know it's scary, but sometimes we have to do things that are frightening to us, that take us out of our comfort zone. Besides, they might not even need you to identify anyone. You're worrying about a *maybe*. I'm worried about you."

"Me! Why?"

"It worries me to see you this upset. I wish I could snap my fingers and make everything okay."

"You could try."

Anthony pulled him close again. "If only I could." He ran his thick fingers through Brett's flaxen hair. "I do love you." He kissed Brett softly.

Brett felt the warmth and love flow into him and his body responded instantly. "Come on."

Maybe it was the tension of the events of the day, maybe it was the heat or maybe it was the fact that tomorrow would be their last day together, but Brett was determined to have his new man as much as he could before they parted company, at least temporarily.

~ ~ ~

Once back at the precinct house, Detective Scott searched for the Medical Examiner's phone number in his rolodex. Hoping against hope that Dr. Driscoll would be there, he punched the numbers and waited impatiently. "Come on! Come on!"

Voicemail.

He slammed the receiver down. "Shit!"

Fingers drumming the stained desk, an alternative sprang to life. "The assistant!"

He grabbed for the Bucks County phonebook. "What the hell was her name? Hardy? Harman?" Then he remembered she'd given him her card. He nervously patted his pockets and found the crumpled three-by-five card. The digits were pushed in seconds.

A somewhat groggy voice answered on the fourth ring. "Yeah."

Scott briefly related the events of the day then asked if she was at the recovery site on Friday night.

"No."

"Do you know who was?"

"Sorry, I don't know that either."

"How can I find out that information?"

"You'd have to ask Doc."

"I already tried him. He's not available."

"Well what do you want me to do?" Although Emily was annoyed by the call, she understood the detective's urgent concern. She took a moment, then restated her last question. "What can I do to help?" Her voice was softer this time.

"Is there any way I can find out, other than asking Dr. Driscoll, who was on that assignment?"

"Yeah, it would be in the report."

"Whose?"

"The coroner's. It has to list all members of the recovery team who were present at a removal. Legal bullshit."

"How can I see that report?"

"It's on the office computer." Emily could hear him breathing and knew what the next question would be. "I'll meet you there."

"Thank you, Miss Hargrove. I'll be there waiting for you."

Emily rose from the couch where she'd been napping and stretched. "Hey!" she called to her boyfriend who was in the kitchen making a sandwich. "I gotta go. Be back a.s.a.p."

He grumbled something unintelligible.

"Ass!"

CHAPTER VIII

EARLY SUNDAY EVENING, May 27th
New Hope, Pennsylvania

Anthony began undressing as soon as the door closed behind them, but Brett stopped him. "Allow me." He pulled Anthony to him and their still-clothed bodies came together, but only from the waist down. Brett lifted Anthony's T-shirt to his neck then he pulled each arm free. Anthony's mouth went dry as Brett's tongue and teeth licked and lightly bit his neck, shoulders and nipples. Anthony trembled with excitement, his heart raced, skin flushed and his knees grew weak.

Brett's head raised up and he locked his mouth onto Anthony's. Tongues darted in and out as the heat welled up between their thrusting bodies. Brett broke the contact, causing his lover to stumble forward, then pushed him onto the bed. Anthony watched wide-eyed as Brett traced a path from his neck to his navel with the tip of his tongue. Anthony's head lolled back as sensations sparked throughout his body. "Oh God!" he moaned repeatedly.

Spurred on by this reaction, Brett slid his heated fingers into the waistband of Anthony's cargo shorts, unbuttoning them and separating the two halves by lowering the zipper. Anthony humped his hips up and felt the shorts slide away.

Brett stopped and took a moment to take in the sight before him. Anthony's chest heaved and his entire body glistened with a combination of saliva and sweat. Anthony's head craned up to see why the passionate tongue bath had stopped. Brett stood between his splayed legs, naked, a condom and lube in his hands. Confused by the apparent role reversal, Anthony tried to scoot back on the bed, but Brett tossed the items aside and grabbed for Anthony's erection through his jockstrap. Ripping it off, Brett greedily took Anthony into his mouth, lowering fully onto the straining shaft. As his lips slid up and down, he ripped open the condom and deftly slid it onto the slick, hard flesh then coated it with lubricant.

Hands clasped behind his back, Anthony watched as Brett, the man he'd known for mere hours, but knew he'd be with forever, slowly lowered himself onto his sheathed erection. Brett gasped at the depth of penetration his act had allowed them to achieve. His eyes locked onto Anthony's, he began to rise, fall and rotate. Time stopped, the world vanished and for those several minutes nothing existed except the two of them.

Anthony rose up, gripping Brett's firm ass, his face contorted in ecstasy. Brett unfolded his legs and wrapped them around Anthony's waist while gripping him by the shoulders. Straining forward, their mouths met as their mutual climax erupted in gasps of passion.

They remained locked together, panting, allowing their bodies to descend from the heights of the passion they'd just achieved. Anthony rolled to his right, topping Brett. Neither man spoke. For a while they lie entwined, staring into each other's eyes. Anthony finally broke the silence with one word. "Wow!"

~ ~ ~

Emily found Detective Scott waiting outside the morgue. He grinned widely in greeting. "Thank you for doing this, especially on a holiday weekend."

"No problem. Come on." Emily swiped her ADT security card through the scanner and the door buzzed open.

Scott recoiled a bit. "Ooh, smells."

"Tell me about it. You really never adjust to the odors in this place no matter how long you work here." She flipped on the lights and continued forward. "The office is this way."

Their footfalls echoed loudly on the linoleum floor as they crossed the large examination room. Scott's eyes darted back, forth, up, and down as they traversed the room. He couldn't imagine what it would be like to actually use some of the medieval-looking instruments on a human body. His mind whirled from the overwhelming stench of death and formaldehyde. He began gagging.

Emily heard the throat clenching sound. "You're not going to hurl, are you?"

Scott shook his head, but Emily could see he was as pale as some of the occupants of the cooler and his face was beaded with sweat. She picked up the pace, wanting to get him into the fresher air of the office. "In here, quick!"

Scott took several long gulps of the air-conditioned atmosphere of the M. E.'s office trying to clear his nostrils of the odor that seemed to cling to his very clothing. Emily, however, was not taking any chances and grabbed a metal trash can, just in case.

"Here." Emily handed him a mint. "This should help." While he sucked on the spearmint-flavored candy, Emily booted up the computer. She scanned the documents and finally located the Craig Jamison file. "Okay, got it."

She scrolled down the report while Scott, feeling somewhat better, looked over her shoulder. "Looks like the Doc took this one on by himself," she said.

"You sure?"

Emily nodded. "Look for yourself. There aren't any other names in the report."

"Who else works here and could have been at the scene?" "Other than me there's Tom Drucker, Sam Ellison and Marge… I don't know her last name. Doc has an additional call list in case none of us is available, but I don't ever remember it being used since he's been the M. E."

"Is it possible he used it on Friday night?"

Emily shook her head. "Nah. He'd have called me or one of the others first before he'd use that list and I didn't get a call that night." She turned to face Scott, whose color had returned. "Sorry."

"That's okay. It was a long shot anyway."

Emily turned back to the computer and was about to shut it down when Scott asked a rather surprising question. "What about the report from Sunday's case?"

"What do you mean? I did that report."

"Yeah, but what about the driver who picked up the remains? Who was that?"

"What difference does that make? I already told you Doc was alone Friday night."

Scott grinned and moved closer to the screen. "Humor me."

Emily exhaled loudly. It was already getting on in the afternoon and she was anxious to salvage at least some of the holiday. She pulled up the Edmunds file. "It was Sam Ellison who picked up the body after I finished my investigation."

She hoped he would be satisfied, but he persisted in asking questions. "What does Sam look like?"

She thought for a moment. "About fifty, tall, skinny, gray..."

"Okay, that's enough. What about the other guy, Drucker?"

"I've never met him." Holding her finger over the power button, she said, "We don't work together."

Scott, dejected by not finding what he'd hoped would be there, nodded and started towards the door. Emily stopped him. "Detective, come back here."

"What is it?" His hopes soared again.

She pointed to the screen. "This." Tapping the liquid crystal display she continued. "This isn't what I wrote!"

Brow furrowed, Scott stared at the screen. "Where?"

"Here." She pointed. "This says that the wound was jagged and caused by a serrated blade, like a hunting knife."

"It wasn't?"

"No! That wound was almost surgical. Clean, like a scalpel made it."

"You sure?"

Emily rolled her eyes and pushed back from the console. "I'll show you. Come on."

As much as Detective Scott did not want to reenter the exam room, let alone go into the cooler, he needed to see the evidence for himself.

Before they left the office, Emily tossed him a few more mint candies. "You never know!"

The heavy metal door strained against Emily's efforts, but finally relented and swung open. There were a few linen wrapped bodies on metal gurneys in the room. "That's odd."

"What is?"

Emily approached one corpse whose coverings were haphazardly tossed over it instead of being wrapped tightly about the form.

"That." She pointed. "When I left here. All these bodies were neatly shrouded. This one's a mess!"

Scott glanced about the chilled room, noting that indeed all the others were tightly wrapped. "Who else has access to this room?"

"We all do."

Scott retrieved his notepad. Flipping the pages he found Brett's description of who he saw the night of Craig's murder. "Does this sound like any of the other male employees? About six foot tall, dark hair, medium build."

Emily thought for a moment, then chuckled. "Almost sounds like the Doc."

Detective Scott almost choked on the candy. "What?"

Emily regretted her off-the-cuff statement as soon as the words left her lips. "Now wait a minute! I said it *sounds* like Doc, but it also sounds like hundreds, maybe thousands of other guys."

Scott barely heard her protest. "Is there a photo of him anywhere around?"

"You cannot be serious!"

"Just find one!" Scott snapped.

Her stomach clenching, Emily led him back to the office and scanned the room. There, on top of a file cabinet was one of the Dr. Driscoll and his wife, Adriana, at a fund raiser for St. Jude's Hospital. "Here." She handed it to him, her hands trembling slightly.

"Thanks. I'll bring it back."

Emily stood, arms folded across her chest as she watched him leave. *Please, God, no!*

~ ~ ~

Dr. and Mrs. Driscoll were in attendance at the annual Memorial Day Gala hosted by New Hope's mayor and held at the prestigious Lambertville House, on the Jersey side of the Delaware. As they waited for the valet parking, he admonished his already tipsy wife. "Please, Adriana, for God's sake, don't embarrass me in front of these people tonight!"

She glared at him. "Always about you!" and slammed out of the car.

"One moment, please. I need to get something out of the trunk." He popped the lid then handed the keys to the vested young man. He retrieved the small package he'd placed there several days ago and nodded to the valet. Catching up with his wobbly wife, he took her roughly by the arm. "Here." He shoved three capsules into her hand.

She stared at the white capsules. "What the hell are these?"

"They'll help you sober up a bit and keep you from having a hangover in the morning."

Mockingly, she replied. "Ahh, aren't you sweet." She popped the capsules.

Driscoll grinned broadly as he watched her choke them down. "You could have waited and taken them with some water!"

Once inside he took her light spring jacket and reached for her purse. She handed over the jacket, but held onto the beaded clutch bag. "My makeup is in there!" She wrenched it from his grip. Adriana was a beautiful woman; pale complexion, dark, almost black hair, sapphire green eyes. Her eastern European father's and Irish mother's genetics had melded together perfectly into this tall, willowy woman before him. *Too bad,* he thought as he checked her jacket. He slid the plastic baggie with the rest of the capsules into the inside jacket pocket then crumpled up the CVS bag. "Could you dispose of this for me?" he asked the coat-check girl who smiled politely and tossed it into the trash.

Taking Adriana by the hand, the couple proceeded into the large banquet room. Driscoll checked his watch. *Soon.*

~ ~ ~

Many of the guests at Raven Hall had gone into town earlier in the day to join in the festivities and planned on staying for the fireworks display. Others, like Brett and Anthony, opted to remain at the resort, wanting to be alone together as long as they could. Many of the others who'd stayed behind did so for a variety of reasons; too crowded, to many kids, too much noise.

"Why does this have to end?" Brett asked as he and Anthony sipped B&B brandy in the half filled dining room after yet another delicious meal.

"What do you mean?"

"This. Here, now. It all comes to an end tomorrow."

"That doesn't mean we have to come to an end!"

Brett grinned. "I was hoping you'd say that." He swirled the warm amber liquor in the snifter, a distant look on his candle-lit face.

"There's something else, isn't there?"

Brett nodded.

"What?" Anthony assumed Brett was still anxious about the earlier interview with the detective, but he surprised him by coming back with, "You live in Brooklyn. I live in Jersey."

Confused by the statement, Anthony asked what that had to do with anything.

"It's the distance. We won't be like we are here, together all the time."

"Brett, even if we lived together we wouldn't be like we are here. We'd be at work every day, at the gym in the evenings."

"I know." He looked into Anthony's dark eyes. "It's just that I'm afraid that when you get back to New York, and life returns to normal, you might, I don't know, forget about me; about us."

"Never! I could never forget about us." He sat back in his chair, a broad smile breaking across his unshaven face.

"What?" Brett asked, not seeing anything to smile about.

"You just made me break the last promise I made to myself."

"Really? And what would that now broken promise be?"

"Never, and I do mean never, be taken in by a hopeless romantic."

Brett chuckled, he'd never thought of himself as a hopeless romantic, but now that it had been said, he had to agree. "Now what?" he asked, his voice softer and calmer.

"We make plans for…"

He didn't get a chance to finish that last statement. Detective Scott had rushed into the room and was heading directly for their table. He was out of breath and panting when he finally got to them. "Here you are!" He took several heavy breaths before continuing. "I've been looking all over for you two."

Anthony and Brett exchanged confused glances. "Why?" Brett asked.

Scott fumbled in his pockets, pulling out the now creased photo of Dr. and Mrs. Driscoll. He held it up for Brett to study. "Is this who you saw Friday night?"

Brett took the picture and examined it, Scott watching him anxiously.

Brett shook his head. "I can't be certain, Detective. It was dark, I was startled by what I'd just seen." He smirked. "And besides, I'd just spent a wonderful evening with the man of my dreams." He handed the photo back. "I am sorry, I just don't know."

Frowning, Scott took the photo back and tucked it away. "Thanks for trying." He started to leave.

Anthony stopped him. "Hey Detective, who is that anyway?"

Without turning, Scott replied in a deadpan voice. "The Medical Examiner."

~ ~ ~

The fireworks display over the Delaware had only just begun when Adriana leaned into her husband. "Take me home."

"Now?"

She glared at him. "Either that or I'm really going to embarrass you!"

"Okay, okay." He fished in his pocket for the coat check slip.

"What the hell are you doing?"

"Your jacket. I was ..."

"Screw the jacket! I can get it tomorrow."

He hurried her through the party, hearing the snide remarks being made by other guests as they passed by.

On the short ride home Adriana's head fell forward, the only thing holding her upright was the seat belt. Driscoll placed his fingers on her neck, feeling for a pulse. *Weak, but still there.*

The garage door swung open, but he left the Mercedes idling in the driveway. He helped his semi-conscious spouse out and had to nearly carry her up to their bedroom. Lying her across the king-sized bed, he retrieved the rest of the capsules from his jacket pocket and spilled some in her purse, others were strewn on the bed.

He began stripping off his suit, but was startled by Adriana's moaning. "Wha happ...?" she mumbled incoherently.

He came to her and stroked her hair. "Relax. You had a bit too much to drink and nothing to eat." He stood and continued changing into jeans and a T-shirt. "I'm going to get us a sub at Wa Wa. You get some rest." He left her immobile on the bed.

He tossed a light jacket onto the passenger's seat, hopped into the car and grinned. *Done!*

~ ~ ~

Emily paced the M. E.'s office. She couldn't believe the detective had actually taken her innocent comment seriously. Her first instinct, after he'd left, was to call Dr. Driscoll, but that would only serve to confirm Scott's suspicions. She fell into the upholstered desk chair and stared at the now black computer screen. Rebooting the system, she pulled up the file on Richard Edmunds again and reread it. Her impulse was to delete the altered phrases and retype them with the correct information, but hesitated. "Damn it!" Frustrated, she shut down the computer and grabbed her purse, leaving the building upset and frightened.

CHAPTER IX

LATE SUNDAY EVENING, May 27th
New Hope, Pennsylvania

Detective Scott sat in his department-issued Crown Victoria at the far end of Raven Hall's parking lot, drumming his fingers on the steering wheel, his mind racing with contradictory thoughts. He finally grabbed the flashlight from the glove-box and bolted from the car. Racing across West Bridge Street, he illuminated the unlit rear parking lot with the wide beam of the powerful light. *They need to put lights back here!* he thought as he treaded cautiously down the embankment to the scene of the second murder. Arching the brilliant beam back and forth, he studied every square inch of ground. *There has to be something we missed.*

He carefully side-stepped down the embankment to the stream beyond, his eyes straining in the fading sunlight. At first, nothing, then a glint of metal caught his eye. He focused the light on it and held his breath. There, under the water was what he knew to be the murder weapon, a physician's scalpel.

"Son of a bitch!" He retrieved the instrument from the chilly water, holding it gingerly by its razor sharp blade and stared at it. He smiled. Once back in his car he radioed the station house. "Get me

Sanders. I need him to dust something for prints!" He didn't wait for a response.

~ ~ ~

Dr. Driscoll thought about his wife and smiled. *She should be gone by now,* he thought. The capsules he'd given her earlier should have done their job, especially since they'd have been combined with the wine she'd drunk earlier that day. Maneuvering his Mercedes west along the twisting roads, he recalled the way he'd obtained the encapsulated cocaine. He had been called to the scene of an apparent drug overdose one Friday night several months ago. As he slid the corpse of a young woman into the black body bag, a small baggie dropped to the floor. He absently picked it up and shoved it into his pocket and proceeded with the recovery. It wasn't until late that evening, while undressing, that he rediscovered the plastic bag. *What the hell?* Then he remembered. *I'll return them in the morning.* He tossed them on the night table, but the plastic slid across the polished surface and dropped behind the table. It wasn't until several weeks later that he noticed the bag wedged there. A lurid grin creased his face and he placed them under the papers on the table. It was then he began developing his plan to rid himself of her once and for all.

Now it was done. *I'm free!*

~ ~ ~

Mike pulled into the parking lot of the Wa Wa across Sugan Street from Raven Hall. Not wanting to be seen, he selected the very last parking place along the side of the building and backed in. The sun was slowly lowering in the west, but he needed to wait for full darkness before he made his move. He went into the convenience store, bought a coffee and package of Hostess donuts then climbed back into his car and got comfortable. *Soon, my fair one. Very soon I will have you!* He laughed as he ate the powdered confections.

~ ~ ~

Dave and Chris fought hard to keep a positive, upbeat outer appearance, but after Detective Scott had the resort locked down and had interviewed several of the guests, their thin veneer was beginning to crack. Pacing the office like a caged lion, Chris asked, "How long do we have to lie to our guests?"

Sitting behind the desk, rotating his chair back and forth slowly, Dave shook his head. "Damned if I know. I guess until they catch the guy."

Detective Scott had told them to fabricate a story that one guest had been mugged in the strip mall parking lot. That he was in the hospital and recovering from the beating, nothing more. "But only volunteer that story if they ask," he'd cautioned them.

Chris stopped and pounded his fists on the desk. "You do know that some of the guys are so frightened by that fabrication that they're leaving early?"

Dave nodded. "I do. But it's better than telling them the real story, isn't it?"

Chris didn't respond to the question. "And that some of them want a refund."

"Chris, honey, sit down." He waited until Chris had perched on the edge of the chair opposite the desk. "There's nothing we can do about the guests who choose to leave. That's their prerogative. The best thing we can do is give them a partial refund and a coupon for a 10% discount on their next visit."

Chris sat stone still on the chair, considering what he's just heard. "That sounds pretty good." He relaxed a bit. "When did you come up with that idea?"

Dave shrugged. "Just now." He looked over at Chris who was now smiling and shaking his head.

"You amaze me."

Dave stood and came around the desk. Standing behind Chris's chair he massaged his lover's chest with his somewhat rugged hands. "Mmm, that feels so good," Chris murmured.

Dave leaned over and gave him an upside-down kiss.

Chris pulled himself to a standing position. He rounded the chair, his lips never leaving Dave's and took him in a tight embrace. "Is the door locked?"

Dave stretched back. "It is now."

Throughout their years together, Dave always had a calming effect on Chris and this situation, thought much more drastic, was no different. Chris let himself be taken then and there. Letting his fears melt away as Dave undressed and entered him. For a while, his fears, apprehensions and worries became as distant as the morning mist over the Delaware.

~ ~ ~

Detective Scott carefully slid the scalpel into a plastic evidence bag. His heart pounded in his ears as he raced back to his car. He sped back to the morgue, hoping to find Miss Hargrove still there, but the building was dark. "Damn it!"

~ ~ ~

Mike carefully picked his way through the small wooded area that bordered Raven Hall. The evening had cooled considerably and he shivered, cursing himself for not wearing a jacket.

From his hiding place, just beyond the stockade fence delineation Raven Hall's property, he waited. He could faintly hear music from the patio bar and the voices of the guests, but could see very little. That, however did not matter since there was only one room in this part of the resort and the only person who'd come this way would be the fair one.

He settled in, a malicious grin breaking on his otherwise handsome face. His thoughts focused on the blond and how he'd meet his end. Mike fantasized, seeing the panic in his eyes, hearing his sobbing pleas for mercy, his screams of pain as he raped him, then, at the moment of climax Mike could almost feel the exquisite quaking of his body as he simultaneously climaxed and slit the fair one's throat. Mike leaned back; he was rock hard and in need of release. His breathing was labored and his arms and legs trembled, but not from the chilled night air.

He closed his eyes and saw the final moments of the fair one's life. *His legs would twitch in death throes, fingers would grasp at the gaping wound, blood pulsing onto the floor, his eyes would bulge as he came to the realization that his life was at an end. Then, slowly, the fair one's legs would quiet, his arms would become still and his eyes would glaze over, their last vision being Mike's grinning face.*

With that last vision fixed in his mind, Mike felt the contractions of orgasm rock his body. Without even touching himself, he'd climaxed.

~ ~ ~

Propped up by pillows on her queen-sized bed, Emily told Tyler, her latest boyfriend, that she didn't want anything to eat, didn't want a drink either. She finally pushed him off the bed. "Ty, please!" Her face was a contorted combination of fear, anger and disappointment.

"Okay, okay!" He held his hands up defensively. "But I'm right here if you need to talk."

She managed a weak smile and answered in a whisper of a voice. "Thanks."

Once alone in the darkening bedroom, Emily pulled her knees up to her chest and closed her eyes. Taking in long, deep breaths, she tried to calm her frayed nerves. It took a while, but she felt some sense of balance returning.

The shrill ringing of her cell phone broke through her attempt at relaxation. She grabbed it off the night table. "Yeah."

Not bothering to identify himself, Detective Scott got right to the purpose of his call. "Sorry to disturb you, Miss Hargrove, but I need you to identify something for me."

Her heart sank and a knot began growing in the pit of her stomach. "What?"

He didn't respond to her question. "Can you come to Police Headquarters?"

There was only silence on the other end of the line. "Miss Hargrove? You still there?"

Emily rubbed the back of her neck. "When?"

"Now."

"On my way." She ended the call, the nervous knot growing as she grabbed her keys and headed out.

"Hey!" Tyler called from the couch. "Where you going?"

"Police Headquarters."

He could see the concern and fear on her delicate features. "Want me to come?"

Normally she'd decline such an offer, but with all that had happened over the past several hours, she nodded. He grabbed his jacket and took her by the hand, comforting her the best he could.

~ ~ ~

Chris emerged from the office, still tucking in his shirt, a faint smile on his reddened face. Dave remained in the small room, reclining back on the sofa that just a few moments ago was the setting for an intense, somewhat rough, lovemaking session. His clothing was still in a crumpled heap on the rug and he groaned as he reached forward to retrieve his pants. He never remembered Chris being so aggressive, but then again they had never been in such an unsettling situation before. He hoped that after all this was over this part, at least, would continue. Dave had always been the dominant one in their relationship and now he was hoping that some of that dominance would become part of Chris's personality. "That would be nice," he commented aloud as he slipped on his loafers. Standing he spotted the photo of he and Chris the day the renovations on Raven Hall had started. He hadn't realized it before, but the past year had aged him more than it should have. He knew there was a seven-year age difference between them, but it had never been noticeable before. Now he could see the effects the stress of the past twelve months had had on him. He looked into the mirror next to the office door and shook his head. *Not good!*

He finished dressing and left the office, his earlier euphoria having been shattered by one, insignificant picture. As he made his way across the covered walkway that fronted the rooms, he saw

Chris. He stopped and watched as he chatted with a few guests and locals. He could hear Chris's laugh as one guest shared a story, the others adding to it, no doubt embellishing the truth a bit.

When he and Chris had first met he'd lied about his age, making himself only two years older than Chris, thinking that would make him more attractive to the young, hot man Chris was and still is. It wasn't until just before their first anniversary that he revealed his true age. Chris's reaction shocked and embarrassed him. "I know."

"How?"

"One night at your apartment in Yardley I saw your college diploma hanging on the living room wall. If you'd graduated on the date listed, you'd have been about fourteen!" He shrugged. "I did the math."

"Oh. I'm sorry I lied, but I was afraid I'd be too old for you."

Chris had taken him in his arms and whispered softly. "You could never be too old for me."

Now he feared he was beginning to at least look too old.

He started walking again, and joined the small group Chris was talking with. Putting his arms around Chris's waist and pulling him n tightly, he began to feel better. Feeling Chris clench his ass cheeks, he began to feel a whole lot better. *Maybe I'm just old enough!*

~ ~ ~

Brett and Anthony had been engaged in conversation by another, older couple. The two couples sat on the patio, away from most of the other guests, enjoying a lively banter. As Brett listened to Al and Joe relate one story after another he wondered if one day he and Anthony would be doing the same with a young couple. He looked over at Anthony's strong profile. *I hope so.*

A fresh round of drinks arrived, wine for Al and Joe, beers for Anthony and Brett. Before anyone could take a sip, Al stood. "Here's to young love."

Anthony looked at Brett and added one phrase. "And to enduring love."

They drank.

~ ~ ~

Emily paced the waiting room of New Hope's small Police Headquarters. "Did he say what he wanted?" Ty asked, his eyes following her back and forth across the worn vinyl flooring.

She shook her head.

"Any ideas as to what he might…"

"Ty!" she snapped. "I do not know!"

He knew when to shut up.

"Ms. Hargrove." The desk sergeant called to her. "Detective Scott can see you now." She buzzed the couple in and directed them to Detective Scott's office. He was standing in the hallway, waiting.

"Thank you for coming in on such short notice. This won't take long. Please." He stood aside and gestured for Emily and Ty to go into his office. Once all three were seated, he handed her the scalpel, still in its clear plastic bag. "Do you recognize this?"

"Anyone knows that's a scalpel."

"Let me rephrase. Is this scalpel from your morgue?"

Emily's jaw dropped. She couldn't believe he was still thinking it was Doc who committed these horrific crimes. Keeping her composure the best she could, Emily replied, "Detective, that scalpel could be from any hospital in the county. Hell it could have come from any hospital anywhere! There's no way to tell."

Scott leaned forward. "You keep an inventory of the instruments used in the morgue?" She nodded.

"Would you mind checking to see if there's one or two scalpels missing?"

Emily rose on leaden feet. Exasperated by the detective's insistence, she groaned, "I'll go check." She passed Ty and walked down the short hall as if in a trance, Detective Scott following them to the exit.

"Thank you, Miss Hargrove. I'll be here, waiting."

Ty sat silently beside his girl as she drove, white-knuckled to the morgue, parking askew in front. "I'll be right out," she said tersely. He watched as she disappeared into the dark structure, one thought repeating in her mind, *he does suspect Doc!*

~ ~ ~

Chris and Dave took time circulating among the groups of men scattered around the resort, socializing and getting to know these people who they hoped would become regular guests. The last evening of a hectic and tragic weekend had both of them energized, exhausted, and frightened.

They ended a conversation with a small group of men who raved about the resort. Beaming with satisfaction, they made their way from the Oak Room to the Patio Bar hand-in-hand. "What are you thinking about?" Dave asked as they strolled along the dimly lit pathway.

"Craig would have loved tonight."

The evening was cool, the sky starlit and, although crowded, conversation in the various bars and near the pool was subdued.

Dave took in a deep breath of the fresh spring air. "He certainly would have."

"Chris! Dave! Over here!"

They scanned the large open space, searching roe who was calling them. After a few moments, they spotted a hand waving in the far corner of the Patio Bar.

Al and Joe had departed, leaving Anthony and Brett to themselves. The owners approached, and after a few minutes of pleasant conversation, Dave turned to Brett. "You okay?" Concern was evident on his face.

"Yeah, I'm okay."

"Good. Detective Scott told us about you possibly seeing the killer and we were afraid you'd be frightened." He turned his eyes to Anthony. "I guess having someone beside you helps."

"That it does." Brett smiled at Dave and Chris and at the same time squeezed Anthony's thigh.

The conversation turned to the upcoming summer and various plans for vacation, as well as the 4th of July.

Anthony wrapped an arm around Brett's shoulder. "I think we'll spend it here." He looked over at Brett. "If that's okay with you."

Brett beamed as he nodded his consent; his fears of earlier having just been wiped away with that one statement.

"Well, we'll leave you guys to enjoy the rest of the evening," Chris said, getting up. They started walking away when Brett called to Chris.

"Before I forget, the light outside my room is out and it's pretty dark down there."

Chris nodded. "I'll replace the bulb in a few minutes."

Dave took Chris by the hand. "See, we done good!"

Chris laughed, the smile lingering on his fair face.

~ ~ ~

"Detective?"

Startled by the sound of a voice, Scott looked up from his desk to see Bucks County's fingerprint expert, Dan Sanders, standing in the doorway.

"Please tell me you were able to get something."

Sanders shook his head. "In the water for that long it's nearly impossible to get a viable print. We did get a partial, but not enough to give us anything of importance. Sorry."

Scott sighed. "Thanks, Dan."

Alone again, Scott found he could wait no longer for Emily Hargrove to report to him, he raced out of headquarters. Placing the red, revolving "bubble gum" light on the roof of his car, he began weaving in and out of the late Sunday evening traffic, navigating the narrow, winding main street, hoping Emily was still at the morgue.

Ty saw the revolving red light reflecting in the dark windows of the morgue. "This can't be good!" he muttered as he got out of Emily's VW Beetle.

Emily was exiting the building when Scott screeched to a fish-tailing stop in front of her. The brightness of the red light caused her to squint. She became cemented to the spot, knowing what she was about to reveal to the detective.

Exiting the Crown Vic, Detective Scott began to ask her a question, but she started talking before he could finish, her voice shaky and barely audible. "I already know. We're three scalpel handles short on inventory."

Scott's eyes popped open wide and his head snapped up. "Three!"

Realizing what that meant, Emily started to break down. Ty pulled her into him, holding her tightly.

Scott nearly tripped over his own feet as he turned to leave. Once in his car he wheeled back out of the lot, radioing headquarters as he one-handed the three hundred-sixty degree turn. "On my way to the Driscoll residence. Send a squad car *now!*"

~ ~ ~

Emily watched, tears streaming down her cheeks as the detective's car disappeared into the night. "He's going to Doc's house. I know he is."

"Em, there's nothing you could do. If he's the one, then he has to be stopped." He lifted her head and kissed each cheek, tasting the salty tears that flowed. "Come on. I'll make you a nice drink and we'll cuddle on the couch, even watch a chic flick. How does that sound?"

Emily couldn't help but grin at that. "Lame!"

~ ~ ~

Detective Scott bumped into the driveway of the stately home, the black and white was already there. Exiting the Crown Vic, he motioned for the officer to go around the back of the premises.

He knocked, then pounded on the solid wood door, ringing the bell at the same time. The home was dark and not a sound could be heard. Scott peered into the double garage; only one car was there; a Cadillac Enclave. "Robbins!" he called.

"Yes sir?"

"His car, what is it?"

Robbins shrugged.

The sound of fireworks caught Scott's attention and he dashed back to the idling car and peeled out of the driveway, leaving Robbins scratching his head.

~ ~ ~

The fireworks display from the Lambertville House could be seen throughout the area, the brilliant colors and the variety of patterns delighting the crowds that filled the parking lot and balconies of the hotel as well as those that lined the main streets on both the Jersey and Pennsylvania sides of the Delaware.

"Come on." Anthony pulled Brett to his feet. A brilliant silver starburst filled the night sky to the east of Raven Hall. The couple stood, admiring the flickering display, Anthony standing behind Brett, his arms wrapped tightly around Brett's tight waist.

The aerial show continued for over an hour, lighting up the late May sky with color. It ended with a barrage of whistles, booms, and explosions in every color of the rainbow. "Now what?" Brett asked as he turned in Anthony's arms and wrapped his hands around his neck.

"Hmm." Anthony grinned and grasped Brett's butt.

They started towards their room, but heard their names being called. It was Joe and Al. "Come join us for a nightcap. Bob Egan is playing in the Oak Room. Sing-along Broadway tunes. You'll love it!"

Brett looked at Anthony who shrugged in surrender.

~ ~ ~

Chris and Dave walked arm-in-arm back towards their private apartment. "Nice people," Dave stated.

"Who?"

"Our guests. No outlandish demands, very few complaints."

"Except for the police presence!"

Dave nodded. "Yeah, there was that. I think we managed to lighten up that situation quite well."

Chris stopped dead in his tracks. "Lights! I gotta do something."

Dave watched as he rushed away, heading for the storage shed beyond the office.

The prefab wooden structure held a hodge-podge of items necessary for the running and maintaining of such a resort; extra towels, table linens, flatware and the like. All were neatly stored in individual Rubbermaid containers.

"Lightbulbs, lightbulbs," Chris repeated as he read labels. "Ah, here they are." He slid the translucent container from its place on the shelf and popped open the lid. He removed two 60 watt energy-efficient fluorescent bulbs, not knowing if one or both of the present bulbs were blown. He replaced the container, turned out the lights and shut the barn-style doors. Even though no one knew when the need for additional supplies would arise, the unit was kept locked. The head of each department - housekeeping, dining, maintenance, landscaping - each had a key and there were several discreetly hidden near the shed in and under planters.

Chris sang softly as he traversed the walkway and bounded down the stairs to Brett's room.

~ ~ ~

As the hour grew late, Mike found it difficult to keep from drifting off to sleep. *Where the fuck is this guy?* he thought as he fought off the sandman once again.

Finally, the clicking of the gate's latch brought him to complete wakefulness. He positioned himself on his haunches on a sturdy tree branch that overhung the stockade fence separating the wooded area from the resort and prepared to strike. Eyes fixed on the small patio, he silently removed the scalpel from its sheath and held it dagger-like in his right hand.

A glint of blond hair registered in his brain and, as the man entered the courtyard, he sprang. Chris heard the rustle of leaves, but barely had time to turn before Mike was upon him. Staggering back towards the far end of the space, Chris dropped the light-bulbs and raised his hands defensively in front of his face.

Mike slashed, the blade slicing into the palm of Chris's upturned hand. Grasping his bleeding hand, Chris tripped on the uneven pavers and fell. He scooted back on his butt as far as the enclosed space would allow, then forced himself to stand. His hand throbbed and droplets of crimson dotted the sandstone patio.

Mike lunged again, his earlier fantasy of a slow, enjoyable rape long forgotten. This was going to be a battle for survival. Chris sidestepped the attack and managed to deliver a punishing kick to the back of Mike's knee. Bounding off the fence, fury in his eyes, Mike slashed again. A scarlet streak blossomed on Chris's cheek, causing him to crumple to the ground in excruciating agony.

It was only then, as his opponent stood with the full moon lighting his face, that Mike realized this blond-haired man was not the fair one he wanted. He knew then that he had to finish this man off as well. Racing at this unknown opponent, Mike let out a banchee scream and caught Chris with a full force kick to the abdomen. Chris mustered up his last remaining strength and kicked the dripping blade out of his attacker's hand.

Mike fell on him and, almost instinctively grasped Chris around the throat and began to squeeze. Chris flailed, striking with his feet and uninjured hand, but it was no use. Within minutes he was unable to fight and his body went limp.

~ ~ ~

Brett and Anthony were enjoying the drink with Al and Joe as well as the entertainment provided by Bob Egan. After a while, however, the room became too crowded and they returned to the Patio Bar. The air had cooled considerably. Instead of sitting, Brett said, "I'll be right back. I want to grab a jacket." He kissed Anthony on the cheek and left.

"He's a very handsome young man." Al said.

Anthony, who was watching Brett, grinned. "Tell me about it."

"I don't know who's luckier, him or you."

His eyes returning to the older couple, Anthony replied, "I am."

~ ~ ~

Mike searched in the darkness for the scalpel, but it eluded him. "Where the hell is that damned thing?" His breathing came in short gasps as his search became more frantic. The latch opened again, and for an instant he froze. Then, leaping onto the bistro table near the rear of the patio, he vaulted over the fence that separated the room from the back of the resort.

Cloaked by the dark curtain of overhanging pine trees, he peered through the slats of the fence to see who had interrupted him. His eyes shifted between the narrow openings, straining to see, but the only thing visible was the blond hair. *Damn it all*! This new man was the fair one!

His fantasy of rape and strangulation rekindled in his fevered brain. He was determined to eliminate this one last problem, after acting out his wanton desires. *Then I'll be free!*

His drive for male sex had been festering for many hours now. At first his desire had been sated by watching various sporting events, especially football. He'd focus his attention not on the game, but on the uniforms and how they clung to the players' tight asses. "Hmm, what I could do with that!" he muttered as he unzipped his pants and took his rock-hard erection in hand. He'd envision what it would be like to penetrate the hottest players, feeling them clench and release their firm butt cheeks as he pounded them harder and harder. He could almost hear their moans and groans of pleasure as he'd climax in a sweaty heap atop them.

The advent of mixed martial arts fighting added another dimension to his fantasy world, that of pain. He would stare, wide-eyed as the two combatants, dressed only in form fitting trunks, would battle. Invariably, there would be a take down and one man would dominate the other, being held by the supplicant's legs in what was called *the guard.* To Mike it was simulated sex. Their sweat-soaked, muscular bodies slid against one another as they fought. The top man moving ever so slightly up and down, pressing his jock encased genitals against his opponents upturned ass. He started imagining himself in the top position, the legs of his conquest wrapped tightly around his waist, but in his version there was no cloth separating the two, no jock straps, no cups, just flesh against flesh.

From there it was only a matter of time before he started searching internet porn sites, graduating from fantasy to video voyeurism.

When those vicarious experiences were no longer sufficient, he began secretly watching men at Raven Hall and other gay establishments in the vicinity. He'd find a parking place in the shadowy recesses of the parking lot and wait. Eventually two men would hook up and begin a heated make-out session. He'd watch as their arousal became evident, releasing then stroking his own erection with one hand while the other pinched hard nipples, driving himself to a nut-busting orgasm.

His desire, his need, to be involved physically with another man, finally won him over, but for some reason he continually found the realities of each encounter not nearly as satisfying as his fantasies. This fact enraged him. Try as he might, none of his tricks could bring him to the same intense and breathless climax his overheated mind could.

He started including light S&M into his encounters, such as spanking, biting and at times slapping and then even punching his partners. This was somewhat more satisfying so he started seeking out men who'd be willing to give in to his violent lust.

However, there was a brief event a long time ago that resurfaced in his conscious mind, causing him to murder.

~ ~ ~

Brett nearly stumbled over Chris's contorted body in the dark. "What the...?" He bent low, trying to focus, then he heard a faint, croaking voice. "Help me."

Brett gasped, finally seeing what he'd bumped into and who it was. Rushing back and opening the gate, he screamed for help.

"Oh my God! That's Brett!" Anthony was on his feet and running in an instant, Al and Joe close behind as were many of the other guests. As Anthony neared the steps to their room he saw Brett. He was unharmed. "Thank God! I thought..."

"Call 9-1-1. Now! Chris is hurt."

Not needing any more information, Anthony pulled his cell phone from his pocket and dialed. Al and Joe arrived. "What happened? You okay?" Al asked.

"I'm okay. It's Chris, someone attacked him. He's in pretty bad shape."

Just then Dave pushed his way through the crowd. "What's going on?" Then he saw Chris lying in a darkened puddle of crimson, his cheek cut nearly through, the palm of his right hand sliced, the blood there already starting to clot. There were also finger-print shaped bruises on his throat.

Dave fell to his knees beside Chris and took his pale, bloody face in his hands. Chris's eyes fluttered open and up to Dave's tear streaked face. "I did, didn't change the, the light-bulbs." Then he fell silent again. Dave cried as he rocked his unconscious liver in his arms. No one spoke, no one moved.

In the distance, the sound of sirens could be heard.

~ ~ ~

Although there was a back entrance that led into the Oak Room, Mike couldn't risk being seen especially with his skin and clothing being splattered with blood. Instead, he picked his way around the back of the resort through the thick undergrowth of ivy that carpeted the ground, climbed up the walls and hung down from the trees, ready to entangle any unsuspecting passers-by. From there he skirted his way along the fence of the far parking lot onto West Bridge Street pacing his way to Sugan Street and finally to the safety of his car.

Once inside the dark vehicle, he lowered the driver's seat, closed his eyes and sank back into the soft upholstery. His entire body shook uncontrollably and his breathing was labored and shallow, heart racing. *Easy now, take it easy. Slow, deep breaths. That's it, in and out, in and out.* His heartbeat slowed, breathing returned to normal and the shakes began to subside.

He replayed the events of the past hour or so, upset by his actions. *He was the wrong man! He was not the fair one.* His only consolation was that he hadn't killed an innocent. *But now he has to die as well!*

~ ~ ~

Detective Scott arrived shortly after the rescue squad. He excused his way through the bystanders, anxiety coursing through his veins. As he neared the scene, the EMTs were wheeling Chris to the waiting ambulance.

"Is he…?"

"No, he's alive, but badly hurt."

Scott looked down at Chris, a man he'd come to like and admire over the past few days, shocked at what he saw. For reasons even he didn't quite understand, her reached out, stroked Chris's bloody, sweat soaked hair and smiled at him. Dave, who'd been walking alongside the gurney holding Chris's hand, took note of the gesture and nodded, understanding its meaning.

Scott stood where he was, watching as the rescue workers secured the stretcher then assisted Dave into the back of the vehicle. All eyes followed as the box-style rescue vehicle, lights flashing, sirens wailing, slowly made its way out of the parking lot, turning left onto West Bridge Street towards Doylestown Hospital, a twenty minute ride away. The crowd slowly dispersed, anguish visible on each face, many crying openly.

The only two left standing there were Brett and Anthony. Scott approached them, taking note of the condition of the small patio area, the overturned table and chairs as well as the blood splatter and pooling. He then noticed Brett's distraught state.

"It's my fault." Brett sobbed.

"Don't!" Anthony held him. "It isn't anyone's fault. Whoever did this is a nut job!"

"But I asked Chris to change the lightbulbs. If I hadn't done that..."

"If you hadn't, it could have been you in the ambulance right now."

Brett gasped. A sudden realization flashed through his mind. "Oh my God! What if that lunatic thought Chris was me!" Detective Scott heard that comment as he neared the men. They saw him and abruptly ended their conversation. "Is there a place where we can talk privately?"

Anthony glanced towards the room, then to Brett, who nodded. Once inside, Brett dropped heavily onto the bed, Scott took one of the chairs by the table, Anthony stood, staying near Brett.

"Mr. Anders could very well be correct. I believe this maniac is after him. That means he's certain you saw him Friday night and can identify him."

Anthony fell onto the bed next to Brett who had scooted up onto his elbows.

Scott continued. "And now. Well, let me ask you this first. Did you see him tonight?" Brett nodded.

"Did he see you?"

Another nod.

"Detective, what are you getting at?" Anthony asked.

Scott stood and paced. "He is now aware of his error. He probably thinks he killed Chris, but isn't certain. You may have actually saved Chris's life."

"But now he's after Brett." Anthony finished the detectives previous thought.

Scott nodded. "I'm afraid that could be a possibility."

Brett spoke for the first time. "Why, though? I didn't see him clearly Friday night."

"He doesn't know that. So if he thinks you did see him he'll be determined more than ever to…" Scott shrugged, not wanting to even say the words.

"What can we do?" Brett was now seated on the edge of the bed, next to Anthony.

Scott fished inside his jacket pockets, pulling out the photo he'd gotten from Emily. "Take a good long look. Is this the man you saw tonight?"

Brett took the now creased picture and stared at it. The longer he took to respond, the more disheartened Scott became.

Handing it back, Brett responded. "I don't know."

~ ~ ~

Dr. Driscoll wheeled the luxury European car into the parking lot of the Cock & Bull Bar and Restaurant in Peddler's Village, just a few miles west of Raven Hall. He sat in the car, windows down, enjoying his first breaths of fresh air as a free man. He grabbed the black nylon jacket, zipped it up and exited the car. He stretched, then started towards the bar entrance. As his sneakers crunched on the pebble walkway, he made a promise to himself. *One drink, then I have to go home to find my beautiful wife dead from a combination of alcohol and drugs.* Holding his hands to his face, feigning shock, he rehearsed aloud in a falsetto voice. "Oh my! She's dead! Boo-hoo!" Pausing momentarily at the door he slicked back his hair and partially pulled the zipper down.

CHAPTER X

MONDAY MORNING, JUST PAST MIDNIGHT, May 28th New Hope, Pennsylvania

During the tedious drive through the narrow country roads to Doylestown Hospital, Chris's facial slash had been treated as had been the cut to his palm. Although both wounds were serious, neither was life threatening. The paramedics were more concerned with the bruising on his throat and torso, saying that they could indicate internal bleeding, although his blood pressure seemed stable at the time.

Dave had not moved, not even blinked since he got into the rescue vehicle. His bloodshot, puffy eyes saw the lines running from plastic bags into Chris's arm, saw the butterfly bandages holding his palm and cheek together, heard the beeping of the machines that monitored his vital signs as well as the wailing of the siren, but none of it registered. He was numb to any and all external stimulus. One thought dominated his entire being as he held onto Chris's uninjured hand: *don't leave me!*

~ ~ ~

Detective Scott left Brett and Anthony after advising them to leave as soon as possible in the morning, fearful that whoever tried killing Chris and saw Brett could still be around, waiting for another opportunity to strike. "He might even try to find you yet again tonight." Scott looked around. "Can you move to another room?"

"I don't know if there's another one available." Anthony replied. "I'll go see."

"Good, that way you'll be safe tonight." Scott bid them good-night and left, softly closing the door behind him.

"Hey!" Anthony nudged Brett who'd drifted off. "Let's see about another room."

Groggily, Brett asked, "Do you still have the key to your old room?"

Anthony shook his head. "Had to turn it in when I moved in here. Come on, get up."

He pulled Brett by both arms, but couldn't budge him. "Honey, come on! We have to get a different room."

"Do we really? I mean, what are the odds of him coming back tonight?"

Anthony gripped him under the arms. "You are not staying here tonight, young man!"

"All right, all right! Let me get a few things from the bathroom."

"I'll go see about another room. Be right back." Anthony stepped out into the patio, but before closing the door told Brett to put the security latch on and throw the dead bolt. His voice muffled by the sounds filtering into the room from the other guests, Brett only heard the phrase; "be right back."

~ ~ ~

Dave watched as the hospital staff rushed to and took the gurney carrying the love of his life into surgery. They'd been notified by the driver of their ETA and were standing by, ready to do what they do best, save lives.

"Mr. Taylor?" a voice called to Dave. "Please come with me." The nurse led him to a waiting lounge in the opposite direction. He craned his neck to keep Chris in view as long as he could.

"Can I get you anything? Coffee? Water?" she asked after seating Dave in the waiting room.

"I could use a bottle of cold water."

She patted his hand and smiled. "Certainly. Anything to eat?"

Dave declined the offer.

After she left, Dave noticed that he was the only person in the large room. The silence was complete, filling his worried brain with its echoing stillness. His eyes darted around the cold, sterile room: white-washed walls, speckled tile floor, green plastic chairs, wall-mounted television that was muted and without closed-captioning, and a rack of months-old magazines. The only sound was the occasional paging of doctors to one room or another, which only served to heighten his anxiety.

The room began to spin and his vision narrowed, darkening around the edges. He felt faint, nauseated and sweaty. He tried to call for help, but his voice failed him, besides, there was no one near enough to render assistance if he could call out. The nurse returned with a large bottle of spring water, a peanut butter and jelly sandwich and an orange just as his body began to go limp and slump forward in the chair. Noticing his condition, she ran to him. With one hand she placed the food items on the chair next to him while supporting him with the other.

His eyes fluttered open and she called his name. "Here, sip this slowly." He took several small sips of the cold water with her holding the bottle. She instinctively took his pulse and felt his forehead. "Feeling a bit better?"

Dave nodded. "Yeah. Boy that was something!"

"When was the last time you had anything to eat?"

"Around... Huh, I don't remember. Hours ago."

"I thought so." She reached for the sandwich. "Here eat this."

"I'm not really hungry."

"I didn't ask if you were." She placed the white bread sandwich in his hand.

Dave finished the small meal in a few gulps then washed it down with the rest of the water.

"How about now? How do you feel?"

"Yeah, I do."

"Tell me the truth. I want to get help and if you're still feeling weak I'll have to lie you on the floor."

"What?"

"I don't need you cracking your skull open on the floor if you pass out." She looked him in the eyes. "Are you feeling well enough to sit up while I hit the call button?" She pointed to the large red pad on the wall just to their left.

"I'm fine." Dave assured her.

Before what was happening could register, Dave was in a wheelchair and whisked into the E.R. His temperature, heart rate and blood pressure were taken and he was given I.V. fluids. He pointed to the bag of saline solution that dripped its contents into a thin tube then into his vein. "What's that for?"

"Your blood pressure was low and the attending thinks you're dehydrated as well."

"What about Chris? Any word on him yet?"

The nurse shook her head. "We'll let you know as soon as we hear anything. Now, try to get some rest." She tucked the sheets in around him, smiled that practiced smile people in her occupation sometimes have, then left, pulling the curtain around his bed.

Panic gripped him. *There's something wrong. They're not telling me everything. Chris...he's gone!*

~ ~ ~

His celebratory drinks downed, Driscoll paid his tab, left a healthy tip and strode back to his car. *They'll remember that!* he mused. As he headed back east, he wondered what he'd do with his new-found freedom. *Of course, I'll have to observe a respectable period of mourning, say a month or so. Then....* He grinned, the possibilities racing through his head.

While he was in the bar, toasting his release from matrimonial bonds, he did made several decisions. First, sell the house, contents and all. Next collect on Adriana's sizable life insurance policy of about one-hundred thousand dollars. Then get rid of both cars, buy a new vehicle, something less pretentious, and start living. He'd take a leave of absence from work, tour Europe, enjoy the good life for a while. Once he'd satisfied his wanderlust, he'd return to Bucks County, buy a small house on a large lot away from the town and people, and return to work until he was eligible for his pension. *A real country gentleman.*

A sense of calm descended over him as he settled into the plush leather seat, the car's engine purring under the hood.

~ ~ ~

Under the cover of darkness, Mike approached room Twelve. He'd watched the dark-haired man leave and heard him say he'd be right back. *I'll have to be quick,* he thought as he quietly opened the gate.

Brett had just come out of the bathroom when he heard light rapping on the door. "You forget your key?" He regretted opening the door immediately. Mike kicked the solid core door, causing Brett to stumble back, sprawling on the floor, slammed the door shut and was on Brett before he could register what had just happened. Straddling Brett across his chest, Mike pinned both arms down to the carpeted floor with his knees. "Hello, fair one!"

Struggling to free his trapped arms, Brett screamed. "Who the hell are you? What do you want from me?"

His voice calm and cold, Mike replied. "I'm your worst nightmare come true and what I want from you is your cock, your ass, and then your life."

~ ~ ~

Anthony waited at the corner of the main bar. One of the barbacks had been sent to find Bob Burns, the general manager, but was having difficulty locating him. Finally, almost fifteen minutes later, Bob appeared. "How can I be of assistance?" he asked, his blue eyes climbing up and down Anthony's trim form.

"I, we need a new room."

"Oh, is there something wrong with the one you're in now?"

"We're in Twelve."

Burns understood immediately and rounded the bar. "Come with me. The room keys are kept in a cabinet in the office."

On the way, Burns asked how his boyfriend was doing.

"He's talked himself into believing that the bastard was after him. He's actually blaming himself for what happened to Chris."

Burns, hearing the tension in Anthony's voice, remained quiet the rest of the walk. Once inside the office, he booted up the computer.

"Is this going to take much longer? I don't want Brett to be alone, just in case."

Burns looked up at Anthony over the rim of his black-framed glasses. "I have to see what rooms are available."

"Wouldn't the remaining keys in that cabinet tell you that?"

Burns shook his head as he found and opened the correct file. "We have several keys for each room, so that wouldn't help. It'll just take a moment or so longer."

~ ~ ~

Brett struggled against his attacker. He used his knees to attempt to dislodge the madman from atop him. "Ooh, a fighter. I like that! You're already turning me on. I'm rock hard. See?"

Mike unzipped his jeans and his hard-on jutted out. He stroked it a few times then grabbed Brett by the back of the head and at the same time thrust his hips forward. "Take it, mother fucker!"

Brett gagged and his eyes watered as the gardened flesh was viciously pounded into his mouth. Mike watched through lust-glazed eyes as his cock slid in and out of the fair one's lips. Without warning, feeling his orgasm building, Mike pulled his erection from Brett's hot mouth. "Oh no, not yet."

Keeping Brett pinned to the carpet with his knees, Mike reached back and undid the belt and zipper of Brett's shorts. "Buck your hips up," he ordered. When Brett refused to comply, he received a brutal back-handed slap across the face. He gasped at the sharp pain and could taste the hot, coppery blood on his split lip. He raised his hips.

"Now you're learning." Mike pushed the shorts down. Grasping Brett's crotch, Mike's eyes widened. "Not hard?"

Brett's face contorted in fury and he glared up into the madman's face.

"I bet you get hard for our boyfriend."

"Fuck you!" Brett spat.

Mike laughed evilly. "No, my fair one, fuck *you!*"

In one continuous motion, he removed one of his legs off Brett, grasped him under the arms and flipped him over, slamming his already bruised face into the carpet, muffling his screams of protest. He pulled Brett up by his sweaty hair. "Quiet, or do you want another slap?"

Brett shook his head.

"Good boy, you are a fast learner." He grabbed both Brett's hands and held them together behind his back. Brett gasped as his wrists were twisted in this awkward position, pain shooting up each contorted arm.

Mike scooted back so that he was now kneeling on Brett's thighs. His eyes focused on the two rounded mounds of Brett's firm ass. He inhaled, "Nice!"

With his free hand he massaged the pale flesh, feeling the tight muscle beneath. He leaned forward, pressing his lips to Brett's ear. "I am so going to enjoy this!"

Brett started losing sensation in his legs when Mike finally moved off them and placed himself between Brett's thighs. Mike reached back with one hand and pushed Brett's shorts to below his knees. "Bend your knees."

Brett tried. "I can't, they're numb."

He twisted Brett's wrists back. Gasping as the new shock of pain coursed through his arms, Brett tried again and was able to bend his knees as ordered. He heard the shorts hit the floor as his legs were pushed apart and a finger probed the deep cleft of his ass, painfully penetrating him.

Brett's heart raced, his breathing was shallow and sweat stung his eyes. He felt tears and his body began to heave with a raw mixture of fear, pain and intense anger. *This can't be happening!* he thought. *Dear God, let him stop, please!* But the torture continued.

~ ~ ~

After what was only a few minutes of searching that seemed like hours to Anthony, Burns found him and Brett another room. He got up, opened the wall cabinet and retrieved two keys. "Room Four, two doors down from here," he pointed.

Anthony grabbed the keys and rushed out.

Shutting the cabinet, Burns said, "You're welcome!"

~ ~ ~

"You must throw one hell of a fuck!" Mike commented as he inserted a second, then a third finger.

Brett began pleading aloud. "Please don't do this!"

"Begging? You're crying, aren't you?"

Brett nodded. "You don't have to do this."

"Oh, but I do. You see, I know you saw me Friday night, didn't you, my fair one? And I cannot let some little faggot identify me, now can I? So you see, you really do have to die." He removed his fingers and sat back, admiring the view. "But that doesn't mean I can't have some fun first, does it? Enjoy you before I off you?" He laughed.

Brett wanted to tell him he couldn't identify him, had told the police he couldn't, but that would do no good now. Tonight he'd gotten a good look at him and could easily describe him to the police. Primal fear coursed through every part of Brett's body, with only one thought repeating, like a mantra, in his mind, *Anthony, please hurry!*

~ ~ ~

Anthony pushed his way through the crowd of now drunk guests and locals. One particularly soused patron turned when Anthony excused himself. "What's your hurry, hot stuff? Have a drink with us."

"No, thank you." He tried to push through.

The sot grabbed his arm. "How about giving me a little kiss?" He leaned in, his breath stale with beer.

Anthony grabbed the man's reedy fingers and peeled them off his arm, bending them back. His lips curled, anger and concern etching his face. "Get the hell off me!" He pushed the man, who stumbled back onto others, spilling their drinks, then he toppled onto the deck. A few men started to protest Anthony's rough treatment of their friend and approached him, but seeing the fury in his eyes they simply parted and let him pass by.

~ ~ ~

For a moment there was silence, then Brett felt something different. He gasped silently, white hot pain shooting into his body as Mike entered him. "You are a tight little bitch!" Brett clenched his teeth against the brutal entry. He wanted to somehow protest, but was unable to move, to do anything against the onslaught.

Finally having the one he wanted, living out his fantasy, Mike soon felt the gathering of his orgasm. He pushed in one final time and released into Brett, collapsing on top of him as the spasms of climax subsided. Brett felt his hands being released a bit and swiftly wrenched them free. Rolling over, he punched Mike in the face, but his blow was weak, his hands having been cinched behind his back for so long. It was enough, however, to shock Mike and cause him to fall back, crashing into the table near the window. Naked, sweaty, and with a look of pure rage on his face, Brett lunged at Mike, turning the tide on his attacker. "You son-of-a-bitch!" he wailed as he prepared to fight for his life.

Just then the door slammed open and Anthony stepped in. At first he was confused by the scene that confronted him. His boyfriend stood on one side of the room, naked, his lip split, and another man, a stranger on the other side, his pants down around his ankles, a condom still in place, both panting. "What the hell...?" he started, but before he could say another word, Brett pointed.

"It's him!"

Suddenly, Anthony understood the situation and started towards the strange man. Mike, his pants already hiked back up and buckled didn't hesitate, he dove through the window, hitting the ground in a glass covered heap. Anthony was conflicted. His instinct was to chase after his lover's attacker, but his concern was for Brett's well-being. He stood frozen in the door frame. Brett made the decision for him. "Get that bastard!"

~ ~ ~

Almost an hour after being wheeled into the ER, Dave was feeling much better. Now, however, he wanted answers about Chris's condition. He pushed the call button and within moments an older, portly nurse arrived. "Feeling better?" she asked as she lifted his wrist and took his pulse.

"I'm fine. How's Chris?"

"Who?"

"Chris Donnely. He was brought in by ambulance just after midnight. How is he?"

"Let me check. I'll be right back."

He watched as she shuffled back to the nurses' station. He could just see her working on the computer. She scanned the screen, then glanced up in his direction. His heart sank. Next she picked up the phone, spoke, listened, and nodded. His heart raced when she got up and, staring right at him, approached.

Standing at the foot of his bed, she related the information she'd received. "Mr. Donnely is out of surgery. His lacerations were sutured and bandaged."

"But?"

She looked at the speckled flooring. "He did have some internal injuries. His spleen had to be removed and he suffered a cracked rib."

As Dave listened tears slid down his cheeks.

"He's heavily sedated, but will make a full recovery; in time."

Dave broke. He buried his face in his hands and sobbed aloud. Part of this breakdown was relief, part was worry.

She came to him and, as a mother would do for her distraught child, took him in her substantial arms. "He'll be okay. You just worry about you."

Dave's sobbing subsided. She lay him back down on the pillows, fluffing them for him. "When can I see him?"

She shook her head. "Probably not until morning. Get some sleep, dear."

"I have to stay?"

She nodded. "At least for a while. You were overwrought and dehydrated. I'm afraid you have to stay, at least for a while."

"What's your name?" he asked as he settled back.

"Lucinda."

He smiled. "Thank you, Lucinda."

She returned the smile then told him once again to get some sleep. "Tell you what, when that saline finishes, I'll have the attending check you out. If he gives the okay, you can leave." She turned out the lights in his cubicle, pulled the curtains and left him.

~ ~ ~

Mike ran, he didn't care where to, he just had to get away. Many of the guests heard the glass shatter and came to see what had happened. Seeing their approach, Mike turned and fled through the parking lot nearest the room. A man had just opened the driver's side door of his Camry.

Mike grabbed the keys, viciously shoved the man to the ground and fled in his vehicle, tires squealing on the black-top. Without the slightest hesitation, he fishtailed left onto West Bridge Street, other drivers slamming to a crunching stop, horns honking, voices screaming.

He pushed the Toyota to its limits, flashing through red lights, careening into oncoming traffic to pass slower motorists in his lane. Finally he spotted a place to ditch the car, a new development across the street from the Cartwheel. There he could get rid of the car and walk back to his own vehicle through the woods to the north of Raven Hall.

At this late hour, most of the homes were dark and since he hadn't turned on the headlights on the stolen vehicle, he was able to glide into a driveway unnoticed. He parked on the far side of a Lincoln Navigator which completely blocked any sight of the smaller car. After wiping down the keys, he tossed them onto the front seat then proceeded to wipe down the steering wheel as well as the door handle. Satisfied that he'd removed all traces of his prints, he began walking back east.

~ ~ ~

Anthony returned to their room to find Brett still naked, cleaning up the shards of glass. "What the hell do you think you're doing? You'll slice your feet and fingers to ribbons!"

"It has to be cleaned up."

"Housekeeping will do that." He grabbed Brett by both wrists. "Stop it!" Brett looked into Anthony's face and cried. "I was…so… scared! He… he was… going to… kill me!"

Anthony held him tightly, letting him release all the anger and terror of the past half hour. Slowly, Brett's tears stopped and he pushed back. "I'm okay."

"You sure?" Anthony refused to let him go.

Brett nodded. "I need a shower. Get the stench of him off my skin." He kissed Anthony and staggered into the bathroom.

Once alone, Anthony fell onto the bed, exhaustion taking him over.

~ ~ ~

Detective Scott arrived shortly after receiving word that another attack had occurred at Raven Hall. He descended the short staircase to room Twelve in one leap. "Dear God!" he exclaimed when he saw the shattered glass strewn over the patio. He pounded on the door.

"Who is it?"

"Detective Scott."

The lock and then the security chain were undone and Anthony opened the door a crack, then seeing it was the detective, opened it all the way. "Come in."

Scott scanned the room, except for the broken window, everything was as it had been earlier that evening. "Where's Brett?"

Anthony pointed.

Hearing the shower running, Scott nodded. "How's he doing?"

"He was beaten and raped. How the hell do you think he's doing?"

Scott was dumbfounded. Then, "You know I'll need to talk to him immediately. I'm sorry." He stood in the doorway, eyes downcast.

Anthony nodded in agreement.

Scott gasped at the sight of Brett's face. There was a cut on the right-hand side corner of his mouth, his cheek was beginning to bruise and his eye was swollen almost completely shut. He had other bruises on his torso and wrists as well. Detective Scott stood speechless, feeling somehow responsible for the events that led to this brutal beating. "Brett, I am so sorry."

Brett's brow furrowed. "For what?"

"For letting this happen to you and to Chris as well."

Sitting on the bed next to Anthony, Brett softly said, "This," he pointed to his bruised face, "isn't your fault. None of us truly believed he'd stay around, let alone strike again!" He took Anthony's hand. "At least I'm still…" He didn't have to finish that statement.

Once again, Detective Scott took the now battered photo out from his jacket. He simply handed it to Brett.

Brett shook his head emphatically, but this time added, "No, this is not him. It looks like him, but…there was something different about the face in this photo. I can't quite put my finger on it, but there are slight differences between the man in this picture and the one who attacked me tonight."

Scott nearly jumped out of his skin.

~ ~ ~

Mike waited for the light on the corner of West Bridge and Sugan Streets to change. Just before it did, a sleek new Mercedes pulled into WaWa parking lot. He'd always admired luxury European autos, BMWs and Mercedes in particular. He crossed the street, watching as the German import glided to a stop in the far corner of the parking lot. Then the driver stepped out. "Well I'll be!" he exclaimed.

He waited for the occupant to enter the store then he silently approached the silver vehicle. Testing the passenger's door he grinned as it opened. He slid in and scrunched down low in the dark interior and waited.

~ ~ ~

"You sure?"

Brett nodded and handed the picture back. "I got too much of a good look at him tonight. I'm almost positive the man in that photo isn't who attacked me."

Scott raked his disheveled hair. "Then I've been building a case on the wrong man!" He headed for the door. "Thank you, Mr. Anders. You've been a great help. I'm just sorry you had to go through this tonight."

Brett grinned, wincing as the skin on his cut lip pulled apart. "I'll be fine, Detective. Glad I was able to help."

Scott came close. "You may want to head to the ER and have a stitch or two put in that. It's kind of deep."

Brett shook his head. "It looks worse than it is."

"Okay then. Good night guys." His voice was warm and almost affectionate.

Once alone Anthony took a close look at the cut. "Nah, it ain't no thing!" Then, seeing the tears in Brett's eyes took him in his arms. "I'm so sorry. Please. I'm sorry." They stood in a warm embrace, Anthony rocking his traumatized lover gently, soothing and comforting him.

~ ~ ~

Dr. Driscoll purchased a turkey and cheese sub and a two-liter bottle of Pepsi, being sure to say that the large sandwich was for both him and his wife, not just him alone. His cordial, outgoing manner endeared the young red-head cashier to him. "Have a good night!" she called as he left.

He hummed as he walked to the car; a huge weight had been removed from his shoulders. He felt light, and for once, truly happy. He tossed the sub and soda into the back seat, he'd dispose of them later, and got behind the wheel.

"Hello, Doc!"

~ ~ ~

Anthony and Brett moved into room Four. It was noisier here, but both men were so physically and emotionally drained they were asleep as soon as their heads hit the pillows. Brett fell into a deep, dreamless sleep, but Anthony was haunted by nightmares. Although his body remained still, his mind tortured him with visions of death – bloody corpses, gaping wounds, ashen bodies contorted and broken.

Each of these hideous visions had one thing in common, they all had Brett's face.

After falling into a fitful sleep, he woke with a start and it took a moment before he remembered where he was. He looked over at Brett, his facial bruising invisible in the dark room, and just stared at him.

CHAPTER XI

MONDAY MORNING,
3 A.M., May 28th
New Hope, Pennsylvania

Detective Scott was angry with himself. "I let one clue determine the guilty party!" He regretted his rookie decision, berating and chastising himself aloud during the ride home. "I'm just glad I didn't have enough evidence for an arrest."

Now he was faced with starting the investigation over, but where and how to start?

~ ~ ~

Driscoll's immediate reaction was to grab the door handle and get out, but as soon as he made a move in that direction, his forearm was gripped with vice-like force. "Oh no. You're not getting away from me this time." Mike pointed to the ignition. "Let's go."

He started the car and backed slowly out of the space. Pulling to the apron of the exit, he asked, "Which way?"

"I think west." Mike pointed left and settled back adjusting the seat to a comfortable reclining position. "Ah, this is nice. That's one thing I always liked about you, Doc. You always had good taste in cars."

"Just how do we know each other?" Driscoll asked, not being able to place the intruder.

Mike feigned hurt. "After all we meant to each other you don't remember me?" He raised the seat and turned to face Driscoll. "Think, Doc. Med school? About fifteen years ago?" He watched as Driscoll's eyes twitched back and forth, then widened.

"That's right!" Mike cackled wildly.

"But…"

"But what? We had a good thing going, you and me. We were tight."

"We were kids!" the M. E. sputtered.

Mike bellowed, his voice echoing in the enclosed confines of the car. "We were adults! We were in love!"

Driscoll grimaced and leaned away as if Mike's voice had slapped him. "We had an affair."

"Oh, is that what it was?" He sat back. "Let's see. We shared a one-room apartment, slept together every night, made love frequently and, what was that last thing? Ah! You were the one who said 'I love you' first. So yeah, I can see why you'd think it was just an affair."

"Be reasonable, Brice."

"Wow, you *do* remember my name! But, sorry to disappoint you, I go by a different name now." He paused, a wicked grin on his still handsome face. "I'm now known as Mike!" He waited until that small bit of information sank in.

Driscoll's head snapped to his right. "You're using my name? Why?"

134

Brice clasped his hands over his heart, fingers entwined. "It's my way of keeping you close. Remembering the good times. Among other things."

"But you vanished after med school."

"And you married some bitch! By the way, how's that working out for you?"

Driscoll avoided answering that question. "It's you. You're the one! Oh God, how could you? What kind of twisted revenge are you practicing? Why?"

Brice sneered. "We always did look alike, didn't we Mikey? People were always thinking we were brothers, even twins."

Driscoll gasped. "You're not!"

"Oh aren't I? That's right my love."

They'd driven past Peddler's Village into open fields and farmland where the darkness was complete. "Pull over. There." Brice pointed to a dirt road that seemed to lead nowhere. "Turn the car off." he ordered.

Driscoll did as instructed then sat stone still, looking forward, both hands gripping the steering wheel. "You didn't have to kill! You could have come to me and we could have talked things over."

"Talked things over! Are you nuts? You ripped my heart out and stomped on it, or don't you remember that?"

His eyes downcast, Driscoll replied. "I remember."

"I wish I didn't."

"Brice." He turned to face him. "Why? I mean what happened to you to make you so angry, so violent? You were never like that."

Brice turned away. "I could never get things back together after we split up. I tried, believe me I tried, but no one ever came even remotely close to being you. The more I tried, the harder it became and my pain turned to anger, then rage. I wanted to get back at you, to hurt you worse than you hurt me." He chuckled. "Even though I'd moved to Dallas I still subscribed to a local Bucks County newspaper. Every once in a while I'd see your photo in it at some event or testifying at a trial, either helping to convict a suspect or free him while I spent my days treating smelly farm hands and my nights cruising the back streets of Dallas." He looked back at Driscoll, his eyes filled. "Some sorry-ass life, huh?"

Driscoll's heart went out to Brice. They'd had a torrid, yet romantic relationship years ago, but he'd ended it, and not well. *"Brice, I can't do this any longer. I've met a woman and I'm going to marry her. You have to understand. I need to have a normal life. My career depends on me being what people want me to be. This relationship won't work, not in the real world. I'm sorry."*

Seated on the edge of their sofa, Brice had quietly listened. He stood and embraced Driscoll, whispering that he did indeed understand. He then walked out of the apartment. He didn't return until the next afternoon, when he knew that apartment would be empty, and only stayed long enough to pack his clothes and leave a brief note: *Gone. Don't know where I'll end up. Took only my clothes. Be happy.*

~ ~ ~

Dave had slept, but only for a short while. When he woke, the IV line had been removed and the other vital sign monitors were switched off. The ER was cool and unnaturally quiet. Through a small opening in the curtain, he could just see Lucinda. He called to her, but she couldn't hear him. He slid from the bed and padded in his stocking feet to the nurses' station.

"Mr. Taylor!" Lucinda called as she saw him approach. "You shouldn't be out of bed!" She came from behind the U-shaped desk and started escorting him back to his cubicle.

"No, no, no! I have to see Chris!"

"I'm certain he's asleep, as you should be."

"I know, but please. I just need to see him for an instant."

Lucinda studied his worry-worn face. "Oh, all right, but only for a moment. Come on." She started leading him to the elevators, then stopped.

"What's wrong?"

She pointed. "Where are your shoes?"

~ ~ ~

Driscoll moved to embrace his former lover.

"Don't!" Brice cautioned. "Seeing you is bad enough. You hold me and it'll only make matters worse."

"What can I do to make it up to you?"

"After this much time? Not a hell of a lot, I'm afraid."

"I am so sorry, but I didn't think that..."

"And there's the problem, Mikey." Brice's anger rose again. "You didn't think, not about me at least. It was always about Dr. Michael Driscoll Medical Examiner, and the hell with anyone else. Tell me something, Mikey, are you faithful to her or do you suck cock on the side?"

He didn't respond.

"I thought so."

Driscoll wanted to leap from the car and run, to get away from this living reminder of what his life had been and the hurt he'd caused along the way to becoming Chief Medical Examiner for

Bucks County. He thought about the two murders and the way the victims were killed. "How did you get the scalpels?"

He laughed sarcastically. "I got them from your morgue."

"What? How did you do that?"

"That's the real genius of all this. I was hired to be a van driver."

"Who hired you?"

"The former M. E."

"Your name isn't on my list of drivers."

"Ah, but it is. It's on your 'on call' list." He could see the confusion on Driscoll's face. "But that list has never been used since you've been the M. E., has it?"

~ ~ ~

Chris slept peacefully. His cheek and hand were heavily bandaged and his face was still pale. Dave stood at the side of the narrow hospital bed, staring at him. Monitors beeped, keeping track of his heart rate, blood pressure and respiration.

Lucinda stood near the door, allowing Dave the private time he needed with his lover. Dave looked over to her. "Thank you," he whispered.

After several minutes, Dave was satisfied and gave Chris a kiss on the forehead and backed out of the room.

Lucinda took him by the arm. "Better?"

He nodded.

"Good. Now back to bed with you. It's past three-thirty in the morning and you still need some rest."

"What about our deal?"

Lucinda nodded. "You get into bed and I'll call the attending. Deal?"

He winked at her.

~ ~ ~

Anthony sat up in bed, unable to sleep. While he watched Brett's chest rise and fall rhythmically, he thought about their earlier conversation about not being able to spend as much time together as they had here, and living a distance apart. With all that had happened over the past three days, he made a life-altering decision. He smiled at his decision, knowing that it was the right thing to do. He gave Brett a quick peck on the cheek and fell back into a restful slumber.

~ ~ ~

"Are we done here?" Driscoll asked.

Brice looked over at him. "I guess. I'm too tired and drained to go on."

Driscoll started the car and wheeled about. "You have to turn yourself in, you know."

"And if I don't?"

His sideways look answered for him.

"You prick!" Brice grabbed the wheel and quickly torqued it to the right, sending the heavy car into a spin. Driscoll backhanded him across the face and he recoiled. "Are you trying to kill us both?" he screamed. He hit the brakes and the German auto came to a stop, sending a huge plume of dust into the night sky.

Brice recovered from the punishing blow and struck back. "Turn me in? Turn me in?" he repeated as his fists repeatedly lashed out.

Driscoll was able to fend off most of the strikes and get in a few hits of his own. "Stop it!" he bellowed.

Breathing heavily, Brice pulled back. "I cannot believe you'd turn me in!"

"For the love of God, Brice, you killed two men! Did you really think you'd get away with double homicide?"

"Actually, I did plan on getting away. Especially since the authorities think you killed them." He smiled. "Remember, I used scalpels from your morgue. Oh, there's also the doppelganger factor."

Driscoll knew that as a stand-by driver, Brice would have been issued and ID and an ADT security swipe card.

"Ha, ha! So you see, sweetheart, they're not looking for me, they're after..." he poked Driscoll in the ribs, "you!"

That shocked Driscoll to the sobering reality of his own dilemma.

CHAPTER XII

MONDAY MORNING
NEARING 3 A.M., May 28th
New Hope, Pennsylvania

Lucinda had kept her promise and the attending physician cleared Dave to leave the ER. He gave her a warm hug. A taxi had been called and he slid into the back seat, staring up at the façade of the hospital.

He arrived back at Raven Hall close to four in the morning. The resort was quiet, no one was hanging around, lurking in the bushed, prowling for sex.

He paid the cabbie and, once he pulled away, stared at the building. The peaceful appearance belied the terror of the previous night. Dave walked towards room Twelve. There was plywood where the window had once been. *What else happened here last night?* he wondered as he took in the destruction.

Returning to their apartment, he hit the shower, running the water hot to ease his aching muscles. After letting the steaming water soothe his body, he dried off and wrapped a plush towel around his waist. He didn't go directly to bed. Instead, he walked through each room, finally ending up in the kitchen. Standing alone in the small room he realized, for the first time, how empty their home was without Chris here. Even if they weren't having a conversation, or even in the same room, with him here the house was filled with the sounds of life.

He sat motionless at the fifties-style table for a moment. His mind and body filled with relief that Chris would be okay, that their lives together hadn't been cut short by a murderous lunatic.

~ ~ ~

The dust settled around and on the car. The two men inside sat staring straight ahead, the only sound being that of the idling engine.

In a dead-pan voice, Driscoll asked. "When did you return to this area?"

"There was a story in the paper about Dr. Martin's retirement, and there, towards the end of the article, your name was listed as his successor. I made up my mind then and there to move back. I didn't know what I'd do when I got here. I just wanted to see you, thinking at first that maybe we could get back together. Then I found out about her!"

"I'd told you about Adriana and that I planned to marry her!"

"I know, but I guess I was hoping you hadn't gone through with it." Driscoll shrugged.

"Anyway, Dr. Martin hired me as an on-call driver..."

"And you started picking up guys, having sex with them then killing them."

"No! At least not at first." Brice related the whole sordid tale of his sexual encounters and their escalating violence, his voice monotone and icy cold. "It's your fault, you know."

"You said that already, but I'll be damned if I let you pin these murders on me!" He put the car in gear and hit the accelerator, dust flying back from all four screeching tires.

Brice panicked. "What the hell do you think you're doing?"

Driscoll didn't answer.

Brice braced himself in the seat. "For shit's sake, take it easy!"

"Scared?"

Brice's breath came in heaving gasps, his eyes widened and his hands fumbled for the seat belt. "I don't want to die!"

"What about those two young men you killed? Do you think they wanted to die?"

Brice's panic stricken face turned towards Driscoll. "You're going to kill us both! Why?"

"You for the murders, me for being such an ass that I let someone like you get me accused of committing them. That makes sense, doesn't it?"

"No!" Brice screamed, "It doesn't. Now slow the hell down!"

"You have the power to save both our lives, Brice."

"How?"

Driscoll slammed the brakes and Brice flew forward, the taut seat belt the only thing keeping his head from smashing into the windshield. "Turn yourself in."

Panting, Brice raised his hands in surrender. "Okay, okay. You win."

~ ~ ~

Brett woke, his bruised cheek and cut lip throbbing. Not wanting to wake Anthony, he slowly slid from their bed and tip-toed into the bathroom. He rummaged through his toiletries bag for his ever-present bottle of Advil. Finding them, he washed down three tablets with water, shut out the light and got back into bed. *Good*, he thought, *I didn't wake him.*

An arm suddenly wrapped around him and pulled him back into a spooning position. "You okay?"

"Fine," he whispered. "Go back to sleep."

He took Anthony's strong hand and held it as Anthony snuggled closer. "You feel warm."

"Well, being this close to you always makes me hot."

Anthony leaned up on his elbow. "No, I'm serious. You feel feverish."

~ ~ ~

Detective Scott tossed restlessly in bed and finally got out. He turned on the television in the family room and tilted his favorite recliner back. At this hour, little more than infomercials were playing, but he wasn't looking for entertainment, he wanted to set his mind free to come up with a solution to his latest problem.

"Warren, come to bed!" his wife of almost thirty years called from the top of the stairs. "It's almost four in the morning."

"I'll be there shortly."

In all their years together she couldn't remember the last time a case had him so distraught. She returned to their bedroom but couldn't sleep herself. She lie in their king-size bed awake and worried. Just as she started to fall back to sleep, she felt the bed being jostled as her husband got back in.

"You okay?"

"I am now," he replied, sounding more like himself.

"Why?"

"I figured out what I need to do. I can't believe I didn't think of it earlier."

She leaned over and put her head on his chest. "And what is it you need to do?"

He told her his new plan of action.

"You're right. You should have thought of that way before now!" She grinned. "Amateur!"

He wrapped his arms around her and kissed her deeply, both of them laughing.

~ ~ ~

Brett sat up and faced Anthony, feeling his cheeks and forehead. "I do not feel hot!"

"Idiot! You can't take your own temperature that way!"

"I can't?"

Anthony shook his head. "Jersey men! No, you can't. Your temperature will be consistent throughout your body, including your fingers and the palm of your hand."

"I did not know that!" Brett was genuinely surprised by this tidbit of information.

"What did you take just now?"

"Advil."

"That should help. If you're still feverish in the morning you might have to be seen by a doctor."

"Don't be ridiculous! Now," he turned back around, pulled Anthony's arm around his waist and pushed his butt back into Anthony's crotch, "Go to sleep."

Facing away from him, Anthony couldn't see the worried look on Brett's face.

145

~ ~ ~

Driscoll headed back east, into town, all the while knowing that he was just as guilty of murder as Brice. *That's different,* he rationalized. As he waited to turn left onto Main Street towards the police station, Brice cautiously unhooked his seat belt. With his right hand on the door lock, he balled up his left hand and struck a crushing blow to Driscoll's face, breaking his nose. In a flash, he unlocked and opened the door, falling out onto the pavement, and ran back west, the only thought on his mind was, *get away!*

His frenetic dash for freedom up the hilly terrain exhausted him within minutes, lactic acid rapidly building up in his calves and thighs, cramping them. He pushed on, slowing to a jog, then to a walk, all the while looking over his shoulder, expecting to see a car screaming towards him at any moment.

Finally, after seemed like hours, he reached his car. His trembling hand unlocked and opened the door and he fell into the dark, cool cabin, panting. *Rest,* he thought, *just for a moment.* He leaned the seat back and shut his eyes.

Back in Driscoll's car, the bleeding from his broken nose started to subside, but the throbbing pain persisted. With one hand he steered the car into the parking lot just to the north of the intersection of Main and Bridge Streets. Once stopped, he flipped down the visor and checked his injury in the vanity mirror. "Shit!" he spat as he saw that the nose was pushed to the left and the skin around his eyes was already starting to turn purple.

CHAPTER XIII

MONDAY MORNING
DAWN, May 28th
New Hope, Pennsylvania

Brice woke with a start. He hadn't intended to sleep and was angry at himself when he saw the sun had started to rise in the east. "Fuck!" He started his Cadillac and left the parking lot. His first instinct was to return to his condo, but instead he turned west, not knowing where he'd end up, and not caring.

As he cruised through the rolling hills of eastern Pennsylvania he chuckled. "I wonder how old Mikey feels!" he said aloud. He glanced in the rear view mirror, the sun was just breaking above the tree line.

He pressed the gas pedal harder.

~ ~ ~

Driscoll had reported the assault to the police then headed to the twenty-four-hour medical clinic south of the town to have his injury attended to. After a brief wait, he was seen by the physician in attendance. The young M.D. asked a series of questions to which Driscoll answered as simply as he could, mostly with one word responses. The doctor took the hint and got to work putting his nose back in its rightful place. A metal splint was taped down the bridge of his nose and cotton strips were inserted into each nostril. "You're going to have a couple of real good shiners there, Doc."

"Don't I know it!"

The attending snapped off the latex gloves and disposed of them in the Haz Mat container. "When you get home, ice. Twenty minutes on, twenty off."

"Can you give me a script for pain meds?"

He nodded and scrawled something on the blue prescription blank. "Take these with food. They will make you drowsy." He looked at Driscoll's battered and bruised face. "And from the looks of you a good long nap wouldn't hurt."

Driscoll hopped off the exam table, thanked the young doctor and started to leave. He paused near the exam room door. "You wouldn't happen to have any of these pills here, would you? The pharmacy won't be open at this hour."

The doctor nodded, left him standing in the waiting room and returned with an amber bottle containing several of the prescribed pills.

"Thanks, Doctor Phillips."

~ ~ ~

Despite the fact that it was a holiday, Detective Scott headed out early. On the way to headquarters on New Street, he phoned Emily Hargrove, knowing he'd get her voicemail. He left a brief message stating that it was imperative that she phone him as soon as she got the message.

The station house was quiet, only a few officers milling about at this early hour. They looked up in surprise when he entered. Officer Compton, the first responder at Friday's murder scene, noted the time on the wall clock, and almost choked on his coffee. "Boy, you're here early!"

"Got an inspiration last night. Come with me." He rushed off to his office, Compton close behind.

He shut the door and explained his new theory to the officer then leaned back in his chair.

"So you don't think it was Driscoll?"

He shook his head. "He wouldn't be so stupid as to use morgue equipment to commit the murders. No, our unsub is trying to make it appear that he did the crimes."

"But wait a minute, why would he be trying to pin the murders on the M. E.?"

"That, my boy, is the million-dollar question."

The room grew quiet as Compton assimilated what he had just been told and Scott waited for Hargrove to call.

~ ~ ~

Driscoll knew he needed to rest, the meds he'd just taken a short while ago already causing him to become drowsy. He couldn't, though, return home. Instead, he drove to the morgue. There he could curl up on the upholstered sofa in his office and get some much needed sleep.

After parking in the rear of the building, he swiped his security card and made his way to his office. He kicked off his shoes and fell onto the cushions. He was asleep in mere moments.

~ ~ ~

Doylestown, Pennsylvania

Brice felt fatigue overtake him, but his desire to put more distance between himself and his crimes drove him onward. Finally, he could not keep his eyes open any longer and turned off the main road at the Doylestown exit. He followed the signs to the center of the small town and found the Courthouse Inn.

The young desk clerk sized him up and down as he registered. When asked about his luggage, he stated that he was staying for the day to rest, refresh and have a good meal and would be on his way later that evening. The clerk was disappointed, but didn't question him.

"The restaurant doesn't open until eight, but there is complimentary coffee, tea and bagels here in the lobby, if you'd like some." He smiled seductively.

Brice glanced over to the sideboard along the far wall. "Thanks. After a shower I just might take you up on that offer." He returned the smile, adding a wink.

Brice took the stairs to the second floor to room 103, tossed the key on the dresser and began to strip out of his stale clothing. *He was a nice little piece of ass,* he thought as he stepped into the shower.

He let the hot water cascade down his body, the heat relaxing his tension-strained muscles. He imagined the young desk clerk naked and splayed face down on the bed and began to get aroused. By the time he stepped out of the shower, he was fully erect. While toweling off he heard a knock on the door. The large, white bath towel wrapped around his waist, tenting out, he unlatched the door and peeked out. The desk clerk stood there holding a tray with coffee and bagels. "You looked like you could use something to eat."

Brice dropped the towel

~ ~ ~

New Hope, Pennsylvania

As was her habit, Emily turned on her cell phone each morning before showering. She started toward the bathroom when the phone buzzed, indicating a new voicemail. *Please don't let it be work!* she thought as she pushed the play button. To her surprise it was Detective Scott. Although she listened carefully, she had to replay the message before she fully grasped the implications.

Pulling her robe around her, she selected the call back feature. As soon as she heard a voice on the other end of the line, she asked, "You sure?"

"Pretty much so. Can you meet me there?"

"Be there in twenty minutes." She ended the call, slipped into jeans a sweatshirt and her Crocs and raced out, her heart thudding in her chest.

Scott nodded and grinned. "Let's go." he said to Compton who ditched the now cold coffee in the trash container and ran out with him. "You think his photo will be there?"

"Has to be."

~ ~ ~

Brett stirred, his fever seemed to have broken, but he was worried nonetheless. Although he'd tested negative the past eight months, and despite his doctor's reassurances that he was in perfect health, he couldn't stop worrying. *One lapse of judgment, one stupid mistake!*

It was shortly after he and Alan split up, he was feeling depressed and sorry for himself. One Saturday night he got dressed in his tightest jeans, a just-tight-enough T-shirt and headed out to take his mind off his defunct love life.

The guy he met that night was beyond hot. Tall, well-built with dark eyes, shaved head and a body to die for, and Brett appeared to be just his type as well. They'd spent most of the evening talking, laughing, drinking and making out in the lounge of Paradise Bar and Motel in Asbury Park, just a couple blocks from the legendary Stone Pony.

As the hour grew later, Brett got drunker. His new friend, Dan, whispered, "I've got a room upstairs. Let's go." Brett teetered to his feet and, laughing at his own state of inebriation, let Dan lead him to his room.

In the morning, Brett woke with a skull-splitting hangover and glanced to his left. "Oh!" he mumbled, turned over and fell back to sleep. He was shocked back to wakefulness a few hours later by being penetrated by Dan's large cock. At first he resisted, still somewhat hung-over and sore, but soon gave in to Dan's morning lust.

A while later, they lie side-by-side, panting. "Man, that was one hell of a way to start the day!" Dan said as he got up and headed to the bathroom. At first, Brett couldn't agree more, but then an icy realization hit him like a sucker punch to the gut. *He didn't use a condom!*

That night still haunts him and he vowed then and there to never let his guard down and have unprotected sex again.

Anthony reached out from beneath the blanket and ran his fingers through Brett's tasseled hair. Brett turned to face him. His eyes still closed, Anthony asked why he was already awake.

"It's our last day together, at least for a while, and I want it to be a long, long day."

Anthony smiled. *If only he knew what I'm planning!*

~ ~ ~

Emily paced the sidewalk, waiting for Detective Scott to arrive. When he finally pulled up, she ran to his car. "What took you so long?" she asked anxiously. He and Compton stepped out of the car. He ignored her question and pointed to the door. "Let's go."

Emily led the two law enforcement officers through the unlit exam room. "Doesn't smell so bad today," Scott commented.

She opened the door to Dr. Driscoll's office and clicked on the overhead lights. Without warning, she gasped and stumbled back into the two officers. She pushed them out as she pulled the door shut. "Holy shit! Doc's in there!"

"What?"

"He's asleep on the sofa!" She opened the door a crack and pointed. Driscoll lie on his side, facing the back of the couch.

"Why would he be sleeping here and not in his own bed at home?"

Emily shrugged. "Probably had another fight with his wife. She tends to drink, a lot."

"We going in or not?" Compton asked.

Scott nodded to Emily who slowly reopened the door. She booted up the computer and searched for the file they needed and opened it. She, Scott and Compton spoke in hushed tones, but woke Driscoll anyway. "You don't have to whisper, I'm awake."

The three of them gasped when they turned and saw the bandages and bruising on his face.

"I look that bad?"

"What happened to you?"

He waved his hand. "Long story. What are you three up to?"

They exchanged glances, then Scott spoke up. "We, or rather I, have a new theory about the killings. We wanted to check something first."

Driscoll stood on wobbly feet. "No need to check anything." He came, barefoot, to the desk. "Em, type in Brice Williamson."

She did as requested. "Who's he?"

"Stand-by driver."

Within seconds, the file appeared, along with Williamson's photo. "My God!" Emily exclaimed.

"Exactly. He's your man, Detective. He's also the one who did this," he circled his index finger around his face, "to me."

Scott and Compton shared a satisfied look. *We have him!* Scott thought.

~ ~ ~

Doylestown, Pennsylvania

Brice relaxed in the king-size bed after Andrew, the desk clerk, left. Propped up on the pillows, he sipped the coffee and munched the cinnamon raisin bagel. *I needed that!* he thought as he chewed. He felt safe, no one chasing him, nobody to hound him, nothing to interfere with his pleasures. This was the first time in a long time he's enjoyed sex for the sake of sex, and it felt good. Maybe his anger towards Doc Driscoll had finally been spent and he could go on to lead a more normal life, find someone and settle down. Maybe.

~ ~ ~

New Hope, Pennsylvania

As soon as he could, Dave returned to the hospital to see Chris. He bought a bouquet of Chris's favorite flower, sunflowers, some magazines, snacks like potato chips, and Combos, his tooth brush, and other toiletries. He peered into the room to see if he was awake before entering, he was still dozing. Dave smiled when he saw how peaceful he looked, but his heart wrenched at the thought of what lie under the white bandages that hid half of his flawless fac. He put the flowers in the water pitcher, since he hadn't brought a vase, then sat in the chair and just watched him sleep. Just being this close to him brought Dave the tranquility he needed. An orderly came in with his breakfast, and seeing him still sleeping, put it on the bed table. "I'll see that he eats when he wakes up." Dave told him.

He glanced under the dome and surveyed the meal. "Oh well, it is a hospital!" he said aloud.

"Dave? Is that you?"

He dropped the dome over the plate and turned to Chris. "Hey you! How you feeling?"

"Like hell!"

Dave kissed him on his unscathed cheek then just laid his head on his chest, listening to his heartbeat. Sniffles told Chris that he was crying. "Hey, what's with the tears?"

Without looking up, Dave told him how terrified he was that he'd never see him again, that he didn't know what he'd do without him in his life.

"I'm still here and I don't plan on leaving any time soon, so relax."

Dave looked up at him. "You have to eat something, sir."

Chris looked at the tray. "I'm afraid to see what's under that chrome dome!"

Dave unveiled the unnaturally yellow eggs, the almost cooked bacon and the toast, which actually looked the most appetizing. "Now eat!" He got off the bed and sat in the arm chair near the window.

Chris mashed up the eggs and, using the plastic spoon, took small bits of them, his mouth unable to open much at all. "Just wait till I get home. You'll pay for making me eat this!"

Dave watched as he took one small spoonful after another. "Not bad. Not good, but palatable."

Dave leaned back in the chair, happy to watch as Chris choked down most of the meal.

~ ~ ~

Driscoll stared at the picture on the computer screen. "People sometimes thought we were brothers."

"I can see why!" Emily commented. Except for the different eye color and the slightly wider face, he *could* be you."

Scott stood behind the two and stared. "Doc, I owe you an apology."

Brow furrowed, Driscoll asked why.

The detective lowered his head. "I was certain it was you who killed those men, especially when we discovered the missing scalpels. I'm sorry."

Driscoll smiled. "That's okay. At least you didn't arrest me."

The whole time they were there, Compton stared at Driscoll's battered face. "That must hurt like a son-of-a-bitch!"

Driscoll took out and shook the bottle of pain pills. "Not with these little babies it doesn't!"

He turned to Emily. "Print out the information on Brice for the detective. That will give him a starting point for the investigation."

"Way ahead of you, Doc." She looked up at her boss, pride and relief evident in her blue eyes.

~ ~ ~

Brett remained sullen and withdrawn throughout breakfast. He didn't want to talk, didn't smile either. Anthony didn't know what to do so he simply let him work out whatever was bothering him on his own. They went down to the pool, Brett still in a funk. Very few people were hanging out yet so Anthony felt he had a chance to talk to Brett, hoping to allay his fears and alleviate some of his growing consternation. When they were finally seated near the pool, Anthony took Brett's hands. "Don't be this way, you'll ruin the entire day for both of us."

"I'm sorry. There are so many things on my mind right now that I'm all confused."

"Well, then talk to me about them."

"Seriously?"

"Of course! I'm not just another ruggedly handsome face, you know. I do have a sensitive side."

"Oh brother!" Brett rolled his eyes. "Okay, here it goes."

Over the next hour or so Brett told him everything that was bothering him from the distance to the one-night stand with Dan. After he finished he waited for Anthony's response. The longer he took to answer, the more fear crept back into his soul.

After several minutes, Anthony smiled and kissed him. "You are crazy, you know that? And to think I broke one of the promises I made to myself for you."

"Which one?"

"Dating a Jersey guy!" He sat up and leaned close. "Look, neither of us knows what's going to happen in the future, hell, we don't even know what's going to happen in the next minute! But, right now and for the foreseeable future I do not want to see anyone else, touch anyone else, kiss anyone else or make love to anyone else. As far as that guy, what was his name? Dave? No, Dan, that was months, almost a year ago, you need to get over that. You are in perfect health and you know it. I'm not going to let you worry yourself gray about something that doesn't exist."

"Wow! I guess I've been told!"

Anthony laughed. "Oh, there is one more thing. I wasn't going to tell you just yet, but I can't stand seeing you like this. I intend to follow you home to, God forbid, Jersey, and see how long it takes me to make it to work from there."

"What are you saying?"

"If I'm going to be living with you, I need to know how long the commute is."

"Whoa! I didn't see *that* coming!"

"You don't want me living with you?"

"Eventually, but not right now!"

Anthony flopped back on his lounge chair. "Jersey men!"

~ ~ ~

Armed with the printout, Detective Scott and Officer Compton left the morgue to begin their search. "Where do we start?" Compton asked.

"The most obvious place, his home."

The sped south along the Pennsylvania side of the Delaware to a newly constructed condo complex.

"Nice digs!" Compton commented as they searched for building 2B.

"Used to be factories in the eighties." Scott told him as they scanned the massive structures for their identifying number. "Sat abandoned for years, then some developer bought them for next to nothing, got wealthy investors and *voila!* You have luxury, high-end condos going for upwards of six figures.

"Wow! Guess I won't be moving in any time soon."

They found building 2B, parked and approached. "His condo is on the second floor." Scott led the way up the open staircase. "Here it is." He rang the bell and knocked loudly on the steel security door. Not getting a response after several minutes, they turned to leave. Hearing a door open they stopped and turned back. A middle-aged woman emerged from the condo next to Brice's tugging a hyper, pint-sized Pomeranian on a pink leash. She asked if they were looking for Brice.

"Yes, we are. Do you know where he might be?"

She shook her head, the little tan dog yapping at them. "Haven't seen him in a day or so. Must be away for the holiday."

"Thank you."

As they continued down the stairs, Compton asked what they should do next.

"We'll check with the DMV through the computer in my office. His car has to be registered. I hope. Then put out a Stop and Hold for it and for him. Let's just hope he hasn't gotten too far."

~ ~ ~

Chris dozed on and off throughout the early morning hours, Dave never leaving his side. Around ten, the surgeon who repaired his wounds knocked then entered the semi-private room. Seeing Dave, he introduced himself. "Dr. Keller. I took care of Chris when he came in."

"Dave. I'm his partner. How is he?"

"Well, let me take a look. He gently touched Chris's arm and called his name, waking him. "Good morning." He smiled at his patient.

"Oh, hi Doc."

"Let me take a look at these cuts, see how you're healing." He snapped on latex gloves then gently unwrapped the gauze bandaging from Chris's hand and removed the absorbent padding. He looked very closely at the wound, checking for any sign of infection. "Good, no reddening, no swelling either. You're already starting to mend. Good!"

Chris's eyes never left the elderly physician's.

"Now let's see how this one is doing." He removed a pair of bandage scissors from the breast pocket of his white lab coat and carefully cut away the adhesive tape from one side of the padding, carefully lifting it up and away from the skin, revealing the repaired cheek.

Dave scooted to the edge of the chair, wanting to see the damage for himself, hoping it wasn't too bad. "How is it, Doc?"

Dr. Keller grinned. "Damn, I do nice work!" He laughed at his own joke, relieving the palpable tension in the room. While leaning in for a closer look, he became serious. "You're lucky he used a sharp instrument, this cut is straight and clean. No jagged, hanging flesh."

Dave grimaced.

Dr. Keller continued, "Any deeper and it could have sliced right through. There was some nerve damage, which will heal, but very slowly." He called for a nurse to treat and rebandage the wounds. He smiled, "You're doing just fine, young man."

"When can I go home?"

Keller thought a moment. "In a few days, probably. You have to let the stitches from these and the removal of the spleen heal a bit more," he said as he checked the scar on Chris's left side. "The ribs will heal on their own. Do you have someone at home to help care for you?"

"Me." Dave responded.

"Then I think you'll be in very good hands.

~ ~ ~

Doylestown, Pennsylvania

Brice slept deeply, adrenaline, tension and good sex putting him out quickly. The room he'd been given was light, airy and sunny. The large windows were open to let in the cool, late-spring breeze. He stirred, then pulled the pale blue comforter over his naked body and rolled over, facing the windows and drifted back to sleep.

He smiled slightly as he slept, believing he'd gotten away, his mission complete. Then his eyes popped open, a knot clenching his abdomen. His thought of elimination the fair one had vanished, but it was replaced with the fear of what Driscoll would do.

He got up and within minutes was dressed and out of the room. He rushed through the lobby, the clerk watching in disbelief as he slammed out of the inn. *There goes the possibility of some afternoon delight!* he thought.

Brice tore from the parking lot and headed back to the main road. Coming to a 'T' intersection, he sat studying the road signs. A grin of satisfaction broke across his face and he spun the wheel to the right, heading south to Rt. 76 and then on to Harrisburg, the state capital.

~ ~ ~

New Hope, Pennsylvania

Scott and Compton returned to HQ and booted up the computer. Using his ID and password, he quickly gained access to the DMV website. "Okay, here we go." He rubbed his cold hands before typing the name.

The screen went blank then displayed a *please wait* message. Scott and Compton stared at the message, willing it to change. "Come on, come on!" Scott hissed. After several moments, the dark screen abruptly changed and displayed the requested information.

Scott and Compton high-fived each other as they waited for the page to be printed out. As the printer worked, Compton commented, "Nice, he drives a 2010 Caddie."

Scott got up, shut down the computer and grabbed the sheet from the printer. Compton followed him into the main room of the small department. "Do me a favor," he said. "Make a copy of this for me then get on the radio. I want a state-wide Stop and Hold issued for this vehicle and for him. Make sure they understand the urgency of the request. Tell them that he's a person of interest in a double homicide and at least three brutal beatings."

Scott paced, hoping another department would see the Caddie and apprehend him, but it was Memorial Day and many departments would be short staffed, officers marching in the many parades planned for the day.

~ ~ ~

Driscoll had returned to the sofa after popping a second Oxycodone.

"Doc," Emily asked, still sitting in front of the computer, "why are you here and not at home?"

Driscoll grunted. "You've met my wife!"

Emily nodded in understanding. She turned back to the computer and was about to shut it down. "Doc? Can I ask you something?"

"Uh-huh."

"Should I correct the autopsy reports on Jamison and Edmunds?"

Driscoll sat up. "What do you mean?"

"Well, look for yourself." She pulled up the reports and pointed out the errors.

"I did some work on the Edmunds file."

"You did? Why?"

"There were some minor errors in the report, mostly grammatical, nothing more. This, though," he pointed to the phrase Emily had shown him, "isn't my doing."

"Who then?" Emily knew the answer to her question.

He didn't answer that, he simply said in a cold voice, "Change them."

She began deleting the altered phrases. "Why would he do this?"

Standing behind her, watching as she typed in the correct facts, Driscoll shook his head. "If I had to guess, he thought that the investigator would assume I changed them to deflect suspicion."

Emily nodded as she finished up.

CHAPTER XIV

MONDAY MORNING, May 28th
Along Rt. 76

Brice followed Rt. 76 westward. In his way of thinking a city like Harrisburg would be the perfect place to lose himself. *I'll be invisible,* he thought. *No one will even notice me.* There was another advantage too, men. The city supported a sizable LGBT community, with bars, clubs, and an active social as well as political scene.

He made sure to set the cruise control. The last thing he wanted was to be pulled over for speeding. He wanted nothing to delay his trip.

Brice saw the state trooper parked on the side of the road, but didn't give him a second thought. Even when he pulled out behind him, his relaxed position behind the wheel remained, as did his smile.

Then the lights and siren started.

~ ~ ~

New Hope, Pennsylvania

Brett couldn't look Anthony in the eye. They lie side by side, reclining in their lounge chairs, each lost in his own guilt. *Why did I react like that?* Brett thought.

I shouldn't have said anything! Anthony chided himself. *I'm such an idiot!*

At just about the same time, they turned to each other. "I'm sorry," Anthony said as Brett told him, "I shouldn't have said what I did." Their words intertwined into unintelligible garble, then laughter broke out as they both felt relief.

"Jersey men!"

"Will you stop saying that?" Brett slapped him on the arm.

Anthony's smile melted its way into Brett's heart. "Okay, I promise to stop."

"Good."

They stared into each other's eyes.

~ ~ ~

Driscoll's cell phone buzzed. He checked the display and rolled his eyes. "Yes, Marion."

"Michael? Where is Adriana? I've called her several times and didn't get an answer on either the house phone or her cell."

"I really don't know where she is. We had a fight last night and she threw me out. Then I got mugged and beaten."

"Oh my! Are you all right?"

"Aside from a broken nose, two black eyes and a lot of pain, I'm fine."

"Then you have no idea where she is."

"I don't have the faintest."

After a brief silence, Adriana's mother asked, "Will you check at the house, see if she's there and how she is? I worry about her so."

As you should, he thought, but replied, "Of course."

~ ~ ~

Along Rt. 76

Brice watched the rearview mirror intently. The trooper stayed behind him, but he kept driving. Then he heard, "Pull the vehicle over!"

He gripped the steering wheel tightly and, after disengaging the cruise control, hit the accelerator. Within minutes the speedometer hit 90 m.p.h. He kept looking behind him, but the trooper was fading fast. "I've got to get off this road," he said aloud. "Get a different car too." He saw an exit up ahead, around a sharp bend. It wasn't Harrisburg, but it would have to do. Hitting the brakes hard he spun off onto the ramp and disappeared from the trooper's view. His senses were primed, and adrenaline poured into his veins. Despite the fear and anger he felt, he was energized by the chase. His smile turned to a grin and he laughed loudly. He was now a wanted man. *This is going to be fun!*

~ ~ ~

New Hope, Pennsylvania

Driscoll knew he could no longer put off the inevitable. "I've got to go," he told Emily and headed home. The house looked menacing as he pulled into the driveway and for the first time since he hatched his diabolical plot, he was frightened. He stared at the front of the home he and Adriana had shared their entire married life. *Here goes nothing!*

He unlocked the front door and, on the outside chance that she had survived the alcohol and drugs, he called her name. Not getting a response, he climbed the staircase, staring at the second floor hallway, waiting for her to leap out at him at any moment. His footsteps echoed throughout the house, making the silence even more unnerving. Finally he reached the door to the master bedroom. It was slightly ajar, as he had left it. He nudged it open a bit more and tilted his head in to get a view of the bed that was against the far wall. She was there, still dressed as she had been the night before, still splayed across the king-size bed, the pills strewn across the comforter and the bottle of wine still on the night table.

"Adriana?" he called. He knew he'd get no response, but something made him tremble at the sight of her dead body. He walked closer. Her skin had paled to the typical ashen hue and her lips were a deep purple-blue. He stood staring at her, not knowing what he felt. Was it guilt?

Was it remorse? Was it loathing? He didn't know. All he knew was that she was dead and he had a responsibility. He picked up the bedside phone and dialed 9-1-1.

~ ~ ~

Along Rt. 76

Brice had no idea where he was heading. The exit he'd taken was for some street, not for a city or town. He pulled off the back road into the parking lot of a Quick Chek. He needed three things – a bathroom, something to eat, and a good map of Pennsylvania. Those things taken care of, he got back into the car and opened the map. "Where the hell am I?" he asked aloud as he scanned the large fold-out map.

He located Doylestown and Rt. 76, then tried tracing his route from there. He looked through the windshield, trying to locate a street name, but saw nothing. He pulled up to the adjacent self-serve gas station and filled the Caddie's thirsty tank. Returning to the store, he paid with his Visa. "Pump two," he told the young cashier.

"Okay, sign here."

As he scrawled his signature he asked, "By the way, what's the name of this town?"

"Phoenixville."

He smiled, thanked her and strode out. *I guess that means the next town is Hooterville!*

~ ~ ~

New Hope, Pennsylvania

The coroner's van pulled into the Driscoll's driveway. Doc led Drucker and Ellison to the master bedroom. "There," he pointed. They worked silently, disturbed by who the victim was and shocked by Doc's battered appearance.

It took a while to complete the process. Photos of the scene were taken, evidence bagged up and the body had to be carefully wrapped in white linen. After all that was accomplished, the remains were gently lifted onto the stretcher, taken down the winding staircase and slid into the back of the black van. "I am so sorry, Doc." Drucker said as he climbed in and started the engine. Ellison said nothing. He'd been friends with the couple for over ten years. He knew they'd had problems in the past and suspected they still did. He couldn't help shake the feeling that things just didn't add up.

~ ~ ~

Scott received information from the State Troopers Headquarters in Ephrata that the suspect's car had been sighted heading west on Rt. 76. The trooper had given chase, but failed to initiate a stop, losing him on the winding road. Scott sighed, "It seems our man has eluded a trooper. He lost him on 76, somewhere east of Harrisburg."

Well, at least we know the general direction he's headed in. That's a help, isn't it?"

"It's the only thing we have to go on right now." He sat up in his chair. "Do me a favor; get a map of this damned state. Let's see what's out there between here and Harrisburg."

~ ~ ~

"What's eating you?" Drucker asked Ellison as they made their way back to the morgue.

"I'm not sure, but something just doesn't seem right with this."

"Like what?"

"I've known Adriana for a long time, even before she and Driscoll got married. I never knew her to do drugs."

"I guess you didn't know her as well as you thought you did."

Ellison shook his head. "No, I knew her. She'd come to me sometimes to talk about the problems they were having. I spent many nights with her crying on my shoulder."

Drucker looked over at him. "Oh really now!"

"Nothing like that! My wife was there and the three of us would talk for hours about what was going on between them."

"I know some about their marital discord, but not that much. What was the real crux of the problem, if you don't mind me asking?"

"I don't want to divulge too much, but let's just say things weren't too amorous in the bedroom."

Drucker nodded. "She didn't want to…"

"No, not her, *him!*"

"Really?"

Ellison nodded. "He'd stay out late many nights, tell her he was working. She began to think he was having an affair with Hargrove."

"Little Emily? No!"

He smirked. "Only Emily vehemently denied that rumor."

"Then who? There's only Marge left at the office and I don't think Doc would be interested in her!"

"Drucker, I didn't say it was someone at work, and I didn't say it was a woman, either."

Drucker took in that little nugget of information. "Oh! Ooh, you're kidding? Doc, with another man!" Ellison nodded.

~ ~ ~

Anthony could no longer sit idle. "Let's do something. I don't want our last day here together to be this dull."

"What do you suggest?"

"Isn't there a flea market on Rt. 29 somewhere?"

"Got me. Want to go for a ride and find out?"

"It beats sitting here."

The Golden Nugget Flea Market and Antique Center had been an institution in the area for several decades. The vendors sold everything from junkyard finds to valuable antiques. You could find almost anything you wanted at one of the outside or inside booths; that is if you wanted to rummage through the piles of items.

Anthony and Brett took their time wandering up and down the aisles, looking, pointing but not purchasing. Anthony asked one of the outdoor vendors if there was a rest room. "In the building," he pointed. "Second floor."

"Be right back."

After using the rest room, Anthony took his time looking through the stalls inside, admiring some of the fine furniture, glassware, china and collectables for sale. One item in particular caught his eye and he inquired about its cost. When he heard the amount, he balked. "Thank you, but no thanks."

"Make me an offer," the man stated as Anthony started walking away. Intrigued, he returned and offered a little more than half the asking price.

The man countered, "How about an even fifty bucks?"

Anthony thought, then nodded. "Deal." He paid and had the item wrapped in newspaper and put into a bag. He left smiling.

Brett saw him approaching. "There you are. What took you so long?"

"Saw something I just *had* to buy!"

"Can I see it?"

"Not just yet." He laughed, then gave in, seeing Brett pout. "Oh all right. It's for you anyway."

Brett opened the bag and unwrapped the item. "Oh my God! I do not believe this!"

Inside the packaging was an original porcelain statue of the first cast of the Broadway production of *Jersey Boys.*

~ ~ ~

Driscoll watched the van with his wife's body disappear around the bend in the road. He wasn't sure if he felt relief or not. He knew that what he needed to do next was not going to be easy and he had to prepare for the shock and drama that was sure to follow. He pulled his phone from his pocket and dialed. "Marion," he started, "I have some horrible news."

He could hear her crying already.

He waited for a moment before continuing, but it wasn't necessary for him to say anything more.

"How?" she asked between sobs.

~ ~ ~

Along Rt. 76

Brice found his way back to Rt. 76 and continued west. He drank the Pepsi he'd purchased at the Quick Chek and tried, unsuccessfully, to unwrap and eat the roast beef sub. "Damn it!" Several miles down the highway he found such a place, one with tables, some snack machines knowing that he'd have to ditch the car soon. After finishing the mediocre sub, he stood and stretched; his back was quite sore. He heard children laughing and turned to see a family of five playing tag in the large wooded area behind the tables. He smiled at the infectious laughter of the youngsters as they bobbed and ran from their parents who feigned at trying to catch them and make them "it".

He looked around and saw their car, a late-model Chevy Lumina. *Not bad,* he thought. Walking towards the vehicle he looked up at them once more, they were so engaged in their game none of them had noticed him. He approached the car and looked it over. *Not bad at all!*

The thought of stealing this, and leaving the Cadillac crossed his mind. He had his hand on the door handle, but stopped, the peal of laughter from the little girl having caught his attention again. He recalled his own childhood, which was sadly lacking in such fun-filled memories, and moved away from the Lumina. *No, not this one. I can't do that to those kids.*

He returned to his own car and took off, watching as the couple's son, a boy of about ten, tackle his dad. The family fell into a laughing pile in the grassy field.

~ ~ ~

New Hope, Pennsylvania

Brett and Anthony spent the rest of the late morning at the flea market, not looking, just walking around. As they headed back to Brett's car, he stopped and took Anthony's hands. "Look, I'm really sorry about the way I reacted earlier this morning. I guess after Alan walked out on me…" his voice trailed off and he shrugged.

"I understand. Maybe I came on a little too strong, but I was serious. I do want us to live together, and soon. Let's talk about it more back at the resort."

"Good."

~ ~ ~

Driscoll briefly told Marion the circumstances surrounding Adriana's death. She heard very little since she sobbed and wailed throughout most of his explanation. "What do you want me to do about the arrangements?"

"I have no idea. I never dreamed I'd have to make funeral arrangements for my daughter! Will you help Sal and I make those decisions?"

His heart went out to her, she was a kind, loving woman and he didn't consider the impact his actions would have on her and the rest of Adriana's family. "Of course. I'll come over this afternoon, if that's all right."

"Yes. Oh my, I have so many calls to make!" She broke down again and the connection was broken.

Driscoll held the phone to his mouth. "Shit!"

~ ~ ~

Dave spent the morning with Chris in his room. By about eleven, he was tired of being confined. "Come on, get in the wheel chair."

Chris didn't argue. "Where are we going?"

"Outside. I saw a courtyard this morning on the way in. The staff was setting up a grill, maybe they're going to barbeque some burgers and dogs."

"Great! Oh, I don't know if I'll be able to eat that."

"No worries, I'll chop it up for you, like baby food." He patted Chris on the head. "Man! You need to wash your hair!"

Chris looked back over his shoulder at Dave. "You can do that later." He sat back and enjoyed being wheeled about. "I could get used to being taken care of."

"Yeah? Well don't!"

~ ~ ~

Driscoll arrived at his in-laws home around eleven-thirty. There were cars parked in the driveway as well as on the street. He parked around the corner and approached the modest ranch house. All seemed quiet as he rang the bell. *This is going to be damned hard!* he thought as he waited for someone to open the fifties-style front door.

A woman he'd never met greeted him and ushered him in. Her eyes widened as she took in the image in front of her. Driscoll's eyes were purple-black and the bandaging was still gaped to his swollen, broken nose. He mumbled something to her and she escorted him into the living room. There was a group of about thirty people, some he knew, others he didn't. Adriana's parents, Marion and Sal, were seated on the sofa in front of the picture window. He paused in the doorway, he'd forgotten how much Adriana and her mom looked alike. Finally he approached the grieving couple. "Marion, Sal, I am so sorry," he said, sitting on the coffee table in front of them.

Marion could only nod, Sal muttered a choking "Thank you."

"My goodness! What happened to you?" Marion gasped.

He briefly explained his run-in with a mugger, not divulging any of the details, then turned his attention to their needs. He took Marion's hands in his own. "What can I do for you?" His tone was sympathetic, but several of those assembled knew of the couple's stormy relationship. They watched him closely.

"Whatever needs to be done," Marion stated, her voice hoarse from crying. "I just can't..."

She broke down again, her husband consoling her the best he could.

Driscoll looked over to Sal. "I'll be sure to get all the arrangements taken care of. Is there anything special you'd like? Flowers? Mass cards? Music?"

"No," Sal stated. "We'll leave all that up to you, if that's okay."

"Certainly." He got up and started towards the door, a few pairs of eyes following him, their start cold and calculating. Once outside he exhaled deeply, *That was not fun!*

From behind the closed storm door, a young woman, Adriana's cousin, watched him.

~ ~ ~

Brett and Anthony returned to Raven Hall to enjoy the remaining hours of their time together. As they walked from the parking lot to their room, they saw Dave coming their way. "How's Chris?" Brett asked.

"Doing well. He may come home tomorrow, Wednesday at the latest."

"That's great! I wish we were going to be here to see him, but we're going to be checking out shortly."

Dave looked around the sparse crowd. "It seems a lot of guys have already checked out." He smiled at the couple. "So things are going well with you two?"

"Yeah, they are." Brett smiled and glanced over at Anthony. "Aren't they?"

"Couldn't be better."

Dave smiled. "Well, guys, if you'll excuse me, I've got things to get done. Will you be staying for dinner?"

Anthony answered for the both of them. "I don't see why not."

"Good," Dave left them to attend to the business of running the resort.

"We're staying for dinner?" Brett questioned.

"You don't want to?"

"Hadn't given it much thought." He took Anthony's hand. "Come on, let's go work up an appetite!"

~ ~ ~

Along Rt. 76

Trooper Ed Mitchell pounded the steering wheel of his cruiser. "Damn it! How the hell did I let that son-of-a-bitch get away?" He patrolled Rt. 76 slowly, searching for any signs of the Cadillac. Finally, just west of Phoenixville he spotted it. A satisfied grin crossed his face as he increased his speed. This time he wouldn't engage the lights or siren until he was mere feet behind him. "Your ass is mine!" he said aloud as he adjusted his position in the seat, keeping his eyes on the rear-end of the Caddie.

Brice was lost in his memories of his childhood and didn't notice the trooper's approach. By the time he did, it was almost too late. He hit the gas and sped off, spewing smoke and road debris behind him. Mitchell kept pace with the high-powered vehicle, pushing his car to its limits. "All officers on Rt. 76, suspect is heading west, just past Ephrata, may be heading towards Harrisburg. Remember, at this time it's a stop and hold, repeat, a stop and hold. I'm lead in pursuit." The grin never left his lips and his eyes stayed focused on the Caddie. Soon he was near enough to conduct a P.I.T. maneuver. His first attempt failed as the large, heavy vehicle fishtailed then straightened out and sped off. He regained his composure and when he was bumper-to-bumper with the larger vehicle, tried again. The Cadillac spun to a dust choking stop, but only momentarily. However, this attempt caused it to stop facing east. Instead of continuing west, Brice sped off back the way he had come.

His adrenaline pumping, Brice began to sweat. "How the fuck did he find me?" he screamed in the confines of his car. He leaned forward, his chest almost touching the steering wheel as his eyes darted back and forth, looking for a possible avenue of escape. He passed one exit then another, hurtling too fast to negotiate the turn-off. The next road sign loomed in the distance and he slowed just enough to make exiting possible. Looking in the side view mirror, he didn't see anyone following him. He sighed in relief. *That was way too close! I've got to get rid of this car!*

~ ~ ~

New Hope, Pennsylvania

"Let me see if I understand what you're trying to tell me." Drucker said as they backed into the unloading bay in the rear of the morgue. "Doc is gay?"

"No, I didn't say that. He might be bisexual."

"That's even worse!"

Ellison didn't answer. They exited the van and removed Adriana's remains.

"Why did he get married, then?"

"Maybe he thought he had to be married if he wanted his career to move forward. I really don't know."

"Wow, you think you know someone and then something like this happens and you realize you don't know them at all."

Adriana's body was removed and rolled into the exam room. "Think he'll do the autopsy himself?"

Ellison frowned. "I don't even think he'll have one done."

"There has to be! State law dictates one in any suspicious or unexpected death."

"I know that. He'll probably simply state in the report that it was accidental, caused by a combination of drugs and alcohol."

"He'll lie?"

"It won't technically be a lie, but yes, he'll lie to make the death appear accidental. And he'll get away with it too."

~ ~ ~

After Driscoll left the Bowne residence, he headed straight to the morgue. *This won't take long,* he thought as he pulled into his reserved parking place. He went directly to his office, bypassing the exam room, and booted up the computer. Within minutes he had completed his report. "Cause of death, accidental drug and alcohol overdose," he said aloud as he typed. Satisfied, he hit the save button and leaned back. It was then that he heard a knocking on the outer door. *Who the hell could that be?*

He approached the door cautiously, then saw that it was one of Adriana's cousins, Maria. He smiled and opened the door. "What brings you here?" he asked as he escorted her in.

She brushed past him. "Let's just say curiosity."

"Oh?"

Maria stood with her arms folded, staring at him. "Tell me what you found during the autopsy."

He was taken aback by her accusatory tone, but tried his best not to show it. "There was nothing to find. No external marks, no visible signs of internal bleeding. I knew she was in good health. There were however, pills strewn across the bed, and a half empty bottle of wine on the night table at the scene. It doesn't take a rocket scientist to figure out how she died. Why are you so curious?"

"I don't trust you. And I don't like you. You put Adriana through hell. You may have fooled my aunt and uncle, but not me, and not some of the others. We were talking after you left. We want an outside coroner to conduct a *real* autopsy.

"No."

Her dark eyes flared. "What do you mean, no? It has to be done!"

"Her next of kin would have to request that. You and your other relatives do not have that authority. Now if you'll excuse me." He moved her to the door, smiling as she walked past him.

"Do not think this is over. We will get what we want!"

He closed and locked the door. *Bitch!*

~ ~ ~

Along Rt. 76

Brice was running in a heated panic. He had no idea what to do now that his original plan had been thwarted. Heading back east was not what he wanted to do, but with one, possibly more, state troopers on his tail he had no choice. "Damn them!" he cursed aloud as the Cadillac took the exit at a high rate of speed. He wasn't able to think straight, couldn't make a decision and not knowing the area didn't help matters any. He made a series of left and right hand turns, hoping one of them would lead to a town. His adrenaline-fueled run left him exhausted. *I need to rest! Stop and think. I can't keep running like this.* Finally he spotted the spire of a church and knew he had to be nearing a town. *Thank God!*

~ ~ ~

New Hope, Pennsylvania

Driscoll returned to the exam room, pulled Adriana's body from the cooler and drew blood for toxicology. "The results of this should satisfy that arrogant bitch!" he stated aloud as he prepared the samples to be sent out to the lab.

There was no need to proceed further and do an internal examination, so he rewrapped the body and slid it back into the cold room.

Now we wait.

~ ~ ~

Maria knew she was within her rights, but Driscoll was correct, she would need the consent of Adriana's parents to have an outside M. E. conduct an independent examination. She formulated a plan as she returned to the Bowne home. Marion would be the hardest to convince, but Sal would be able to make her see the necessity of having an outsider examine Adriana's body. *Not that it would prove much.* Maria knew all too well that one M. E. would never contradict the findings of another, let alone when a spouse was involved. In addition, it was a well-known fact that her beloved cousin did have a serious drinking problem. "Here goes nothing!" she said as she pulled into the now empty driveway.

~ ~ ~

Dave was surprisingly relaxed throughout the remainder of the day. He'd taken care of much of the daily business of running the resort and found time to have a late breakfast, he hated the word *brunch!* He returned to the office to get a head start on some of the kitchen's orders for the upcoming week. His thoughts wandered to

Chris and how his face would be scarred from the attack. When Dr. Keller removed the bandages, Dave got a good look at the scar. It would require some plastic surgery, but on the whole it didn't look too bad. He was relieved, for Chris's sake. One thing Chris prided himself on was his flawless, creamy white complexion, now that was gone forever. *He might like the new, rugged look!* Dave laughed. He didn't care, he'd love Chris no matter what, just as long as he was alive.

He settled down to work. "Why the hell does Chef need so many radishes?"

~ ~ ~

Anthony and Brett lie together after making love. "It's at times like this that I wish I hadn't quit smoking," Anthony said.

"You smoked? How long ago did you quit?"

"I guess close to five years ago. I started having a nagging cough every morning and sometimes at night. Then there was the cost. They'd gone up to almost ten bucks a pack in Brooklyn. I couldn't afford that. So I threw out the pack I had in my pocket and never picked up another cigarette again."

"That's great!"

"What about you? Have you ever had to give up something you liked?"

Brett nodded. "Sure did. Food."

"What?"

"I used to be huge, close to two hundred fifty pounds."

"I don't believe it!" Anthony said as he looked Brett's naked body up and down. How did you drop the weight?"

"I call it D and E."

"And that stands for?"

"Diet and exercise."

~ ~ ~

Along Rt. 76

The exit Brice took led him to a bridge that crossed over the Schuylkill River. Even though there were no troopers visible, he maintained a speed of over seventy miles per hour. He careened onto the roadway, causing other motorists to swerve to the left in order to avoid a collision. He resettled himself in the leather-trimmed seat and, without signaling, cut across the three lanes of traffic into the far left passing lane. He eased up a bit on the gas pedal as his car melded into the crowded holiday travelers. Up ahead, the traffic was coming to a complete stop. "Fuck!" he pounded the dashboard, "An accident!"

Without hesitation, he pushed his way into the immediate right lane, then moments later edged over once more. *Just in case.*

Once cleared of the three car pile-up the roadway opened up and he once again sped into the passing lane, but this time he kept his speed to just above the legal limit. He didn't know it, but he'd already been spotted.

~ ~ ~

New Hope, Pennsylvania

Maria spoke softly, but firmly to Marion and Sal, a few of the remaining relatives adding their nods of agreement to her plea. "We'll all rest easier if we know the truth."

Sal saw the wisdom in her argument, but Marion refused. "No!" she bellowed. "Is it not enough that my daughter, my only child is gone! Must you now use her death to take revenge on a man who was your lover?" Her swollen, bloodshot eyes fixed on Maria who was physically struck by the accusation.

"My lover! Him? Never!"

"Yes, Maria. You and my daughter's husband."

"Marion I swear to you…"

"I know of your late night visits to their home and of you staying overnight in the guest room. Adriana's neighbor has told me of such things."

"Yes, but did she tell you about the reasons for my visits?"

Marion brushed off Maria's attempted explanation. "Don't even try!"

"No, Marion, I was not there for him. I was there to console Adriana. She'd call me, crying, on nights when he'd leave her alone while he went out searching for sex somewhere else. For sex with," she lowered her head and voice, "men."

Marion slapped her. "Liar!"

"Marion!" Sal grabbed her wrist. "Adriana is gone and Maria only wants to help. Stop this!" Marion fell onto her husband's shoulder. "Forgive me, Maria."

She came to her aunt's side and took her hand.

Marion looked into her niece's dark eyes. "Please, for me, don't do this thing. Adriana's gone. Let her rest."

Maria nodded. *He's won.*

~ ~ ~

Alone in the house, Driscoll sat at the desk in his home office, a Dewar's and soda in his hand. He took out the insurance policy on Adriana and scanned it over. They'd taken out hefty policies on each other shortly after the wedding. *"It's for your protection,"* he'd told her and he partially believed it at the time. Now, however, he'd be the one who'd reap the benefits.

How strange life is, he mused as he read the policy. It stated in no uncertain terms that he was the sole beneficiary and stood to gain the entire amount of the policy. He tucked the document into the top desk drawer and left the room, sipping the scotch as he went.

~ ~ ~

Brett and Anthony stirred after spending time talking about their past and the people and events that led them to be the men they were today. Brett finally got up and headed to the bathroom, leaving Anthony sprawled across the queen-size bed. He watched as Brett strode away. *Damn that's nice!* He rolled over onto his stomach and rehashed their conversation. He'd never really gotten to know any of his former lovers as intimately as he now knew Brett.

Maybe that's why they all failed after a few short months. He shook his head and let it sink into the soft, downy pillow. Soon he drifted into a semi-sleep state, a contented smile on his face.

Brett let the hot water soothe him as well as clean his body. He couldn't wait to get home and tell Pamela about the weekend, focusing on Antony. A warmth surged through him as he thought about spending the rest of his life with him. *A man couldn't ask for more!*

~ ~ ~

Along Rt. 76

Brice believed he had eluded the troopers and relaxed behind the wheel. He turned on the radio and sang along with Tina Turner who was Rolling Down the River. A road sign caught his eye and he made a split second decision. *Delaware! I'll head south to Delaware.* Behind him, in an unmarked car, an Ephrata cop radioed this latest information to the State Troopers patrolling this stretch of highway.

Trooper Mitchell had made it a personal quest to be the one to stop and possibly take Brice into custody, and after being informed of this latest development, quickened his pace and set out to stop Brice's interstate run. "He won't make a fool out of me again!" he said aloud. They were still quite a distance from the state line and it was his plan to end Brice's attempt to escape justice. He grinned, anger curling his lips.

~ ~ ~

New Hope, Pennsylvania

Maria left her aunt and uncle, disappointed with the outcome of her visit, but understanding their desire to have the matter settled. She headed in a familiar direction, but not towards home, she pointed her car towards the Driscoll residence.

Driscoll was in the midst of making a late lunch when the doorbell rang. Licking mustard from his fingers, he was surprised to see Maria standing there. He blocked the entrance and gave her a, *what do you want?* look.

"May I come in?"

He stood aside and waved her in. "I'm making a sandwich, so if you don't mind…"

She followed him into the large, modern kitchen.

Her eyes took in the spacious room. "I always loved this room. Adriana did a good job in decorating it." She ran her manicured hand over the smooth granite-topped island.

"You didn't come here to compliment the décor of the room. What do you want? I'm hungry."

Her arms folded she told him in an icy voice, "My aunt and uncle do not want to further their grief. They've asked me to let the matter drop."

He took a bite of the salami and cheese sandwich. "Smart people."

"This does not mean I agree with them, but I will honor their wishes."

"How magnanimous of you!"

"Don't be so damned smug! I'll be watching you very closely."

"You can let yourself out."

She turned on the heels and slammed out of the house.

~ ~ ~

Along Rt. 476

Brice merged onto Rt. 476 to Delaware then, in a split second decision hooked onto Rt. 40, heading to Newark. "New Ark," he pronounced it aloud. "Kind of like a new beginning." He set the cruise control at sixty-five m.p.h.

As the primary in the pursuit, Trooper Mitchell knew he could follow the suspect across state lines, but he radioed his office none the less. "HQ, suspect has crossed over into Delaware. Continuing pursuit." He waited on the soft shoulder for a response.

His radio crackled to life. "Delaware state troopers and local law enforcement agencies will assist," he heard. "You remain primary."

"10-4." He pulled back onto the highway, his eyes straining to locate his prey.

Brice slowed as he entered the city. He'd been on the run along unfamiliar highways and was beginning to feel fatigue set in. He pulled into an Exxon station that had a 7-11 attached. He filled the car then headed into the small convenience store. He purchased a bottle of spring water and a Snickers bar. "Is there a motel nearby?" he asked as he paid.

"Yeah, about five or six miles south," the cashier pointed to his left. "A Motel 6."

"Thanks." He walked swiftly to his car, watching the scene, alert for any police cars and pulled out into traffic, glad that he'd be able to rest and get a good meal soon.

He found the motel and parked the dusty Caddie facing a low-lying landscaped berm located on the side of the motel.

"And how long will you be staying with us?" the young brunette asked, her smile a dazzling white.

"Only overnight."

She completed the registration form, swiped his Visa card and handed him the key. "Room 10, last room on the right. Is there anything else?"

"Yeah, is the restaurant open?"

"Of course. It's right across the foyer." She pointed straight ahead. Brice nodded his thanks.

Mitchell scanned the highway. Nothing. "Damn it!" he spat. "Where the hell could he have gotten to?" His training kicked in and he mentally went through the list of things a fugitive might need; food and fuel being at the top of the list. With that in mind, he began a systematic search of the service stations along this stretch of highway.

~ ~ ~

New Hope, Pennsylvania

There'd been no word from any state or local law enforcement agency over the NCIC since early morning, and Detective Scott was getting anxious. He sat at his desk, fingers tented in front of him, staring at the phone, willing it to ring.

Compton had stayed with him, seated at the edge of the rickety arm chair opposite the detective. "This waiting is nerve wracking!"

Scott chuckled, not moving a muscle.

"I mean, how long can he keep going? He has to stop somewhere, sometime, even if it's just to take a piss or gas up!"

Scott gasped. "That's it!"

"What?" Compton watched as Scott suddenly sprang into action, booting up his desktop. "This just might help," he said as he typed furiously.

Compton came around to see what his boss was up to. He smiled, "Of course!"

~ ~ ~

Along Rt. 476

Trooper Mitchell stopped at every convenience store and every service station on both the west, then eastbound lanes along Rt. 476, showing the photo he'd printed out from his on-board computer to every attendant and clerk. He asked the same question of them all and got the same response, "No, haven't seen him."

Finally he heard something that made his heart race. "Yeah, he was in here."

"When?"

"Oh about an hour, hour and a half ago."

"Which way was he heading when he left?"

"I can't say, best bet is towards Newark."

"Thank you." Mitchell got back into and started the car. "Suspect last seen near Phoenixville, heading east." He resumed his pursuit with renewed vigor.

~ ~ ~

New Hope, Pennsylvania

Using the tracking book issued to all county law enforcement agencies, Scott was able to pull up Brice's recent credit card usage. He scrolled down the page, scanning for the latest entries. "Here!" he said, pointing. "Phoenixville."

"Where's that?" Compton asked, still hunched over his shoulder.

Scott referred to the large wall map of the Keystone state. "Southwest of here. He was there about two hours ago. He could be heading to Harrisburg."

Compton pointed out the intersecting highways leading to the two neighboring states. "He could be trying to get out of the state as well, either to Jersey or Delaware."

Scott nodded. "Send this latest intel out over the wire service now."

"Yes, sir, right away."

~ ~ ~

New Hope, Pennsylvania

Dave left Burns in charge and returned to the hospital just before noon. Chris was up and walking in the hallway, a male nurse helping him. He saw Dave and grinned, then flinched as the pain in his healing cheek flared. "Hi sweetheart!" he said.

Dave kissed him on the lips, not caring who saw or what they thought. "How you feeling?" he asked as he ran his fingers through Chris's freshly washed hair.

"Not too bad. The ribs hurt more than anything, especially when I laugh or take a deep breath."

The three resumed walking, Dave to the right, Sean, the nurse, holding onto Chris's left arm.

"You holding up okay?" Sean asked.

Chris nodded.

"You don't want to overdo it."

"I know. Just once more up and down the hall."

"Okay, but then you need to rest and have lunch."

"Ugh! Do I have to?"

Sean scowled, "The food is not *that* bad." joshed

They completed one more lap of the long corridor then returned to Chris's room. Once he was settled in an arm chair, as he refused to spend the day in bed, Sean smiled and left. Dave's eyes followed Sean as he strode out of the room.

"Hey! I'm over here!" Chris scolded.

"Sorry. Nice kid!"

"Yeah, right!"

The lunch tray arrived, its aroma caused Chris to gag. He lifted the dome and grinned, "Oh goodie! Soup, a roll and Jell-o, yum!"

Dave shook his head. "Shut up and eat!"

~ ~ ~

Brett's anxiety grew with each tick of the clock. He wanted time to stop, for him and Anthony to be caught in a time loop from Friday till now over and over again forever, but he knew the reality, the clock would continue droning on, the day would draw to a close and they'd leave, each returning to his own life.

They'd laid on their backs atop the comforter, enjoying just being together. Somehow after such a short period of time filled with so much intimacy, words seemed unnecessary, the touch of their bodies saying more than mere words could express.

Anthony stretched and turned to Brett, draping an arm and leg over him.

"Hey!"

"What? I thought you liked having me all over you."

"Yeah, I do, but I like to breathe also!"

"Oh." Anthony moved his arm onto Brett's chest, gently pinching one nipple.

After a moment, Brett asked, "When will I see you again?"

"I don't know." Anthony replied, his voice dream like. "How about Friday night?"

Brett smiled and turned to face him, reaching between his legs.

"What? Again?" Anthony asked, laughing.

~ ~ ~

After sending out the latest intel, Scott and Compton again played the waiting game. "Man I hate this! I'm 'bout as nervous as a virgin in a whorehouse."

Scott looked at him. "What the hell did you just say?"

Compton shrugged, "I'm from Kentucky!"

Scott laughed and repeated the expression. "I have *got* to remember that one!"

A short while later, Officer Sanders knocked then entered Scott's office, a satisfied smile on his face.

Scott knew immediately what that meant. "Really?" he jumped up.

"Yes, sir. A match. The prints do belong to Williamson. The thumb print we got off the scalpel was identical to the one on file with the county."

"Great work, man!"

Sanders left the paperwork with the detective and backed out of the uncomfortably warm room.

Scott got on the wire and sent out this latest bit of incriminating evidence necessary to arrest Williamson for murder.

He sat back after finishing, sweat breaking out on his forehead. He closed his eyes and took a few deep breaths. *Doc is in the clear!*

~ ~ ~

Along Rt. 476

With the suspect's last known location and the new information, Trooper Mitchell knew he was definitely heading to Delaware and that he could now arrest this guy on murder charges. His desire to be the arresting officer stemmed from an overwhelming need to be recognized, to gain the approval of his superiors and his demanding father. He'd been sickly as a child and never lived up to his parents' expectations. He went into law enforcement to prove his worth, but so far over his three-year stint as a trooper he hadn't managed to achieve the goals he'd set for himself. *I'll show them this time!* He thought as he made his way to the Delaware state line.

He implemented the same stop-and-ask procedure he'd used to get this far and it wasn't long before a clerk at an Exxon station told Mitchell that the suspect had been there.

"Where was he heading when he left?"

"Said he wanted a motel to rest. I told him about the Motel 6 just ahead."

"Thank you." Mitchell ran from the store and sped off. On the way he radioed the local police as to the suspect's possible location. He finished by stating, "Do not apprehend! Surround and secure the premises only!"

This is it! He thought as a satisfied grin cut across his freckled face.

~ ~ ~

New Hope, Pennsylvania

Dave stayed until Chris told him to leave. "I'm tired and you need to get back to the resort. You *are* in charge, you know."

"You sure you want me to leave? I can stay. I left Burns in charge."

"Burns! All the more reason you need to get back there!"

"Okay, I'll be back later."

He came to Chris and kissed him deeply. "Love you."

"You too. Now get!"

Chris watched him leave then slid out of the chair and into the bathroom. He loosened the bandaging on his cheek and, with trembling fingers, lowered the gauze and raised his eyes to the mirror. "Oh God!" he exclaimed.

~ ~ ~

"I'm going to need the next few days alone." Brett stated as he and Anthony unraveled from each other.

"What for?"

"To heal!"

They laughed. "I guess the sex is okay…" Anthony started.

"Okay! You call what just happened *okay!*" Brett began poking Anthony in the stomach and ribs, causing child-like laughter to fill the room. When they'd calmed down, Anthony kissed him. "I do love you, very much."

Stealing a line from one of his favorite movies, *Ghost*, Brett simply replied, "Ditto!"

~ ~ ~

Driscoll hastily made arrangements for Adriana's funeral. He selected a high-quality coffin, knowing that her insurance would pay for it and that he would get a sympathy discount from the undertaker.

He knew he wouldn't be able to collect on the policy until the toxicology report came in, which could take up to six or seven weeks. It didn't matter, there was no rush to cash in on her untimely death. He had other things to attend to in the meantime.

He sat in his home office and began writing a "to do" list. It included calling the Good Will to take Adriana's clothing and jewelry, contacting a local real estate agent to list the home for a short sale, and visiting a car dealership to trade in both vehicles. *Maybe I'll pick up a new Hyundai Sonata, they're pretty nice.* He folded the paper and put it in the desk, next to the insurance policy.

"I'm hungry!" he stated aloud, his voice echoing in the empty house. He grabbed his keys and headed out.

~ ~ ~

Brett pulled Anthony to his feet. "Come on, we haven't eaten yet today and I'm starving!" Brett started dressing, but Anthony just stood there. "Anthony! Get dressed!"

"Doesn't this joint have room service? I'm drained!"

Brett tossed him his shorts. "Good choice of words, and yes, they do, but let's get out of the room for a while, see if anyone we know is still here."

"Oh, all right!" Anthony moaned and began dressing.

The bright early afternoon sunlight caused them both to squint and shield their eyes as they stepped out of the darkened room. Brett turned the "do not disturb" sign over to read "maid service required". The lovers strolled hand in hand down the walkway towards the dining room.

"There's Joe and Al," Brett noted and called to them.

"Well," Joe said, looking at his watch. "About time you two lovebirds showed yourselves!"

Brett blushed, Anthony grinned like a Cheshire cat.

"Come on, join us. We're going to be leaving soon."

Anthony let Brett go ahead of him, "You go ahead, I'll get drinks. What do you want to eat?"

Brett thought. "I'll leave the decision up to you." Anthony nodded, a bit surprised, and left, the cat-like smile lingering on his lips.

"I take it things are going well?"

Brett smiled. "Almost too well."

Al asked what he meant.

Brett shrugged. "He's almost too good to be true. I keep holding my breath, waiting for a bombshell to drop."

Joe shook his head. "Don't do that to yourself." He moved closer. "I'm going to tell you something he said the other night."

Brett leaned in.

"I asked him who he thought was luckier, him or you."

"What did he say?"

"He said he was!" Joe sat back. "He's totally devoted to you, so just forget about any stupid bombs dropping!"

Brett smiled and sat back. Then his eyes widened. "What the…"

~ ~ ~

Delaware

Mitchell pulled into the entrance of Motel 6. There were several local law enforcement vehicles already there. He instructed them to take up strategic positions, effectively surrounding the building, one black-and-white was situated behind the suspect's vehicle, boxing it in.

He approached the front desk, his demeanor one of a man on a mission. The clerk stared, instantly alarmed by his swaggering approach. "How may I help you, officer?"

"Trooper Mitchell, Pennsylvania State Police. Is this man registered here?" He handed the printed photo to the clerk.

"Why yes, he is. Came in a while ago."

Mitchell's fingers twitched and he felt a surge of adrenaline. "What room is he in?"

The clerk punched in the name. "Room 10, last room on the right."

Mitchell thanked the young woman and exited the building. "Room 10, he told the officers who had assembled at the front entrance. Get there now and wait."

Mitchell re-entered the building and, after getting a key for the room, carefully made his way down the carpeted hallway. The local officers surrounded the corner room careful not to be seen through the large window on the back wall.

One officer crawled under the window and peeked through it. His jaw dropped. "He's not there!" he said in a hushed voice to the others.

"You sure?"

He glared. "Yes!"

Mitchell knocked on the steel fire door, but got no response. Using the key he'd acquired from the clerk, he opened and entered the room, gun drawn. One look around and he holstered his revolver. "Fuck!"

Brice had been in the restaurant when Mitchell and the others arrived. He watched them closely, then when they'd all gone to the rear of the building he made his way out through the front exit. Sliding along the building's façade, he made his way to the car, but found a cruiser parked behind it. He grinned, *stupid,* he mused as he got in and punched it. The Caddie bumped and pitched over the berm, lopping off several of the rhododendrons and azaleas planted there. He wheeled back around the mound and, with tires squealing, bolted onto the highway.

Mitchell heard the commotion outside, then saw the other officers scramble. He didn't need to see or hear anything more. He streaked back down the hall, crashed out of the door, and was back in pursuit within moments, the others following.

~ ~ ~

Along Rt. 476

Brice sat at the edge of the seat, fingers clamped on the steering wheel in a death grip. Weaving in and out of the mid-afternoon holiday traffic he constantly checked the rear-view mirrors. *That was way too close!*

He considered continuing south, but when he saw an "Official Use Only" turn-about, he instinctively spun the car through it, heading back north, cutting across traffic, causing a five-car pile-up in his wake.

Mitchell heard the sound of squealing brakes and crashing metal and saw the smoke rise. "That bastard!" he spat through gritted teeth.

Jersey dividers had been erected along the length of the highway, so he had to continue south until he came to the same turn-about Brice had used. Engaging the loud speaker feature of his radio, he assured the people in the accident that help was on the way, then he hit the lights and siren to clear a path and accelerated after the wanted man. *He's racking up a hell of a lot of violations!* His eyes seeing only the black Cadillac, he reached speeds of upwards of one-hundred m.p.h., catching up with him in moments.

"Pull the vehicle over!" he called in the speaker. His demands fell on deaf ears as Brice pushed his faltering car to over one-hundred ten.

Mitchell kept pace, but realized innocent civilians could be hurt or worse. Brice had already shown his callousness by causing one accident. Then to his shock the Cadillac cut across the four lanes of traffic to an uphill exit ramp. "He's crazy!" Mitchell screamed aloud. He slowed and merged right, watching the black shape hurtle up the ramp. "He'll never make the curve at that speed!"

~ ~ ~

New Hope, Pennsylvania

Detective Scott and Officer Compton sat glued to their chairs. There'd been no bulletins forthcoming since the one about finding the suspect at a Motel 6.

"I don't know how much longer I can take this suspense!" Compton said.

"Waiting's a bitch, ain't it?"

A voice from the radio receiver broke the trance-like silence in the room. "Suspect located, heading north on Rt. 476 towards either New Jersey or back to Pennsylvania."

Scott edged closer to the set, hoping for more, but there nothing more came through. "At least we know they're on his ass! It won't be long now." Scott checked his watch. "We might actually be able to salvage some of this holiday yet!"

Compton grinned. "Sure!" The sarcasm evident in his voice.

~ ~ ~

New Hope, Pennsylvania

"What is it?" Al asked, his eyes following Brett's stare. "You look like you've seen a ghost."

Brett stood. "Worse! Look over there."

Al and Joe saw the man Brett was indicating. "You know him?"

Brett nodded. His blood ran cold as scenes of the attack resurfaced in his mind, panic gripping him. He wanted to run, to hide, but his body was stone, cemented to the spot.

"Brett!" Al called and tugged on his arm. "What's wrong?"

Brett snapped back to the present. "I think that's the guy who..." He touched the scar on his lip.

~ ~ ~

Along Rt. 40

Mitchell watched the scene unfold in front of his shocked eyes as if in slow motion. The luxury American auto tilted then fell over to the passenger's side. It broke through the steel guard rail, rolling over and over down the steep embankment, plumes of dust, rock, and car parts hurtling in all directions. Other drivers fishtailed and swerved to avoid the debris as the two ton projectile streaked their way. Finally the crumpled remains of the car came to a rocking rest on its roof, the flattened tires spinning as if still trying to get away.

From below, Mitchell could only watch in horror as the drama ended. "Holy Mother of God!"

~ ~ ~

New Hope, Pennsylvania

Scott paced, the waiting was even getting to him. Finally the words they wanted to hear for hours now came through. "Suspect down. I repeat, suspect down."

Scott and Compton cheered. They high-fived each other, their smiles unerasable. "Now that son-of-a-bitch can stand trial," Scott stated as he dropped wearily into his chair. But then their moment of celebration was sobered by the following statement. "Suspect is expired."

The room went silent, the air sucked from it.

~ ~ ~

Along Rt. 40

The two northbound lanes of Rt. 40 were closed as the debris, the destroyed Cadillac and the body of Brice Williamson were cleared from the roadway.

Mitchell stayed in control as the various state and local agencies did their work as quickly and efficiently as they were able to. Within ninety minutes only the soft shoulder remained closed and the several mile back-up began to clear.

Mitchell approached the EMTs who'd bagged and removed the body. "Pretty gruesome, huh?"

"It was. He was broken in several places and a piece of metal had sliced through his neck. Messy!"

Mitchell looked at the black bag that held the remains. *Justice,* he thought.

~ ~ ~

New Hope, Pennsylvania

Scott started heading to Veteran's Park for the annual PBA barbeque. As he neared the intersection of Main and Bridge Streets, however, a thought flashed into his mind and he swung the wheel sharply to the right. *They need to know,* he thought.

Within several minutes he was pulling into the main entrance of Raven Hall. He pulled right up to the front of the main building and parked askew, behind two vehicles. He got out, leaving the door open, and scanned the area, looking for Dave. His jaw dropped when he saw Dr. Michael Driscoll talking and laughing with a handsome young man, periodically touching him seductively. "Well I'll be…" he said as a stunned grin crossed his face.

He heard his name being called from a distance and looked to his right to see Brett frantically signaling to him. Keeping an eye on the M.E., he went to Brett. "What's up?" he asked casually.

Brett pointed. "There, that's the man who attacked me!"

Scott looked to see Brett was pointing to Driscoll. "No, Brett, it isn't. The man who attacked you and Chris and who murdered Jamison and Edmunds is himself dead."

"What? No! That's him, right there!"

Scott fumbled in his stretched out jacket pockets. "Here, remember this photo?"

Brett nodded. "How can I forget it?"

"Now take a look at this print out."

Brett stared in disbelief as he held the two pictures side-by-side. "I don't believe it! These guys could be brothers!"

"I know. That almost caused the wrong man to be arrested. Luckily it didn't come to that. So rest assured that man over there is not the one who attacked you. He's lying dead in a morgue somewhere in Delaware."

"Delaware!"

"Yup, that's where he was found and that's when he made the mistake of trying to escape from a very persistent Pennsylvania State Trooper."

"Did the trooper shoot him?"

"No." Scott related an edited version of the story to Brett. "So that ended his reign of terror. I just wish it had happened sooner." He looked down at the deck, his eyes distant.

"Detective, you did all you could with the little evidence you had." Brett said with his hand resting on the detective's back.

Scott looked directly into Brett's eyes. "Thanks. You were a major part of the investigation. If it hadn't been for you he might still be on the prowl."

"Glad I could help."

Scott again looked around. "Have you seen Dave? I want to tell him the news."

Brett pointed. "I think I saw him heading into the office a little while ago."

Scott thanked him again then added, "You're healing well. Take care and good luck with Anthony." He smiled, shook Brett's hand and left.

Anthony arrived with two plates holding Cuban Paninis. He stopped, looked at Brett, Joe and Al, each looking into the distance, as if watching an invisible movie. He glanced behind him, hoping to see what they did, but there was nothing there. He turned back to face them, a perplexed look on his face. "What did I miss?"

~ ~ ~

Scott found Dave in the office and, standing in front of his desk, informed him of the recent developments in the case.

"Wow! Really?"

Scott nodded and sat, the look of satisfaction glowing on his lined face.

Dave leaned back and sighed heavily, then tears began to flow.

"What's wrong?" Scott asked, alarmed by this unexpected reaction.

Dave waved him off while he regained his composure. "Aah, sorry. It's just relief I guess. That and sadness for Craig and Ed."

"And Chris." Scott added. "By the way, how is he doing?"

Dave smiled. "Coming home by week's end."

"That's great! Well," Scott stood. "Now you guys can enjoy your resort and not have to worry any longer." He extended his hand.

Dave took his rather large, rough hand and held it tightly. "Detective, thank you so very much for all your help."

Scott nodded and turned to leave. He stopped at the door. "I hear the food here is pretty good."

Dave smiled proudly. "Award winning!"

"I'll have to bring the wife here for dinner one weekend."

"Please do so, your meals will be on us." Scott smiled and left.

~ ~ ~

Driscoll saw Detective Scott walking his way. His immediate reaction was to hide, but Scott had already seen him.

The detective waved and smiled as he approached Driscoll and his young companion. "Will you excuse me for a minute?" Driscoll walked towards Scott, smiling. "Detective! What brings you here?"

"I was about to ask you the same question, Doc."

Driscoll stuttered, his face beet red. "I...I..." he started, then, staring Scott right in the eye asked, "Do I really have to tell you?"

Scott shook his head. "Just don't let your wife find out!" He hadn't yet heard of Adriana's demise. He then informed Driscoll of the recent events in the murder case. Driscoll became sullen and Scott could see tears form in his eyes. "He was more than a friend, wasn't he?"

Driscoll exhaled, "Yeah, he was."

"Why did he..."

"Revenge. He felt I jilted him for Adriana."

Scott nodded. "What a shame that he thought he had to do something so drastic."

Driscoll nodded.

Scott looked over Driscoll's shoulder. "You'd better get back to your friend before he finds someone else."

Driscoll glanced back. "Yeah."

Scott began walking to his illegally parked car. "See you, Doc."

~ ~ ~

Joe and Al finally said their good-byes, packed up and left, Brett and Anthony watching as they pulled out of the parking lot.

"You think we'll be together for thirty-plus years like them?" Brett asked.

Anthony looked quizzically at him. "Are you always going to be this pessimistic?"

"I just worry, that's all."

He slung an arm around Brett's shoulders. "Don't. I'm not going anywhere, except back to Brooklyn later today, that is."

Brett put an arm around Anthony's waist as they headed back to the nearly empty Patio Bar. "Idiot!" he laughed.

Once seated, side by side, Anthony became serious. He took Brett's hands in his own and looked him in the eye. "Listen to me. I know you're guarded, and I understand the reason why. I would be too, but I promise you that I'm yours and yours alone for as long as you want me." His voice cracked as he continued. "I've waited so long to find the perfect man and you, Brett Anders, are him! You know, I keep seeing our future, dreaming about it, and it's a wonderful one. Not perfect, but pretty damned close to it. And so with all that's happened over the past seventy-two hours I swear to you, here and now, to love, honor and cherish you always."

By this time tears streamed down Brett's cheeks. His blue eyes reddened. "Oh boy! You really know how to get to me!" He wiped the tears away and smiled as widely as the cut on his lip would allow.

Anthony pulled him close and held him, feeling the slight trembling in his body. "I love you," he whispered.

"And I you."

CHAPTER XV

MONDAY EVENING, MAY 28th
New Hope, Pennsylvania

As the afternoon melted into evening, Raven Hall regained its serenity. The ancient stand of white pines that bordered the pool stood tall and proud, guarding Raven Hall from the outside world. The surface of the pool rippled gently in the early evening breeze. The hibiscus continued to dot the area with their bright blooms.

Few guests remained and even fewer locals were to be found. Conversation in the Main Bar was hushed and the Oak Room was closed. Only three tables in the large dining room were occupied and most of the wait staff was cut for the evening.

Dave stopped to talk with each table of diners, his pleasant, outgoing personality returning as the trauma of the weekend began to fade. He left the diners to enjoy their meals and casually meandered through the grounds. He stopped at the far end of the pool, nearest West Bridge Street and looked back at the resort, his eyes surveying it from left to right. He smiled continually as the low-wattage lights accented the walkway, the rose-lined path and the two-story Patio Bar. *This is good!*

EPILOGUE

MARIA

For several weeks, Maria kept the threatening promise she'd made to Driscoll. Either her or another member of her family kept a suspicious eye on him day and night.

Near the end of August her brother, Steven, came to her. "Maria, this is senseless. He's done nothing suspicious. Maybe it is time for you to reexamine your motives and for the suspicion and hatred you harbor for this man."

Maria despised him and still believed he had a hand in Adriana's death. "All right", she finally conceded, "we'll stop." She slumped into her living room sofa, her chest heaving. *You have won, Doctor Driscoll... for now!*

DETECTIVE SCOTT

Detective Scott and his wife had become regular diners at Raven Hall, enjoying a meal at least twice and sometimes three times a month, as well as the unique personalities of the men and women they'd come to know.

"Why haven't we eaten here before?" she asked one Sunday evening as they drove home.

"It's a long story. Let me just say I was being a fool."

"Ah!" she put the pieces together and knew the answer to her question. "That's all right, dear." She patted his thigh. "We all live and learn."

Ain't that the truth!

DOCTOR DRISCOLL

Dr. Driscoll didn't follow through with many of his original plans. After Adriana's funeral, at which Marion had to be helped through, her grief inconsolable, he gave most of the insurance money to the Bownes. "Are you sure about doing this?" Sal asked. "This is a lot of money!"

Driscoll couldn't bring himself to look the grief stricken father in the eye. "She was your daughter. You and Marion deserve to have it." He finally glanced up into Sal's teary eyes. "Do something special, something in memory of Adriana. Please."

He did sell the house and the cars, but couldn't bring himself to buy a Hyundai. Instead he purchased a 2012 Buick Lacrosse. "American made!" he proudly boasted as he drove out of the dealership.

The condo he now occupied became his sanctuary. Although located at the southern-most edge of New Hope, it was secluded enough to allow him the privacy he wanted. He entertained periodically, hosting both elaborate dinner parties as well as intimate suppers for two. He kept a somewhat low profile, Maria's warning echoing in his head, but found ways to meet men and satisfy his needs. *Maybe there is someone out there for me.*

CHRIS AND DAVE

Chris returned home Thursday, Dr. Keller making him stay an extra day to be sure his breathing was okay due to the cracked ribs.

He had the bandages removed and started occupational therapy to regain usage of his hand and functionality in his cheek. Plastic surgery to lessen the visibility of the facial scar was scheduled for after Labor Day, when the resort would be quieter. Dr. Keller was right, he *did* do nice work!

Life for Chris and Dave settled into a pleasant routine of doing what they loved to do, accommodate their guests and make them feel more like family. None of the locals ever mentioned the tragedies of Memorial Day, not to Chris and Dave or any of the guests who stayed at the resort. "It's none of anyone's business!" Mother had said one afternoon. "They're here to enjoy the resort, not to hear stories about what happened." She laid back in her lounge and sipped her drink. Sadly, Mother passed shortly after Thanksgiving.

The resort was still running a bit behind their expectations financially, but they were in the black, barely.

Chris was still self-conscious about the facial scar, despite the fact that it was barely visible. "Everyone's looking at it!" he told Dave repeatedly one busy Friday evening.

"Chris, they're only looking at it because you keep calling attention to it by covering it up constantly! I swear, no one notices it at all!" He took Chris by the arm. "Please relax about it. Soon enough the plastic surgeon will make it disappear!"

Chris grinned. "I don't know if I *want* it to disappear. I kind of like it a little."

Dave threw up his hands. "I give up!"

BRETT AND ANTHONY

The Friday after Memorial Day found Brett pacing his apartment like a tiger in a cage. He'd rearranged pillows on the sofa, straightened an already straight painting and constantly looked at his watch and out the picture window facing the main drag.

"Where is he?" he fretted. Anthony had called over two hours ago, stating that he was just leaving work.

"You have the directions?" Brett asked anxiously.

Exasperated, Anthony replied that he not only had Brett's meticulously hand-written directions, but that his car had a GPS system. "I'll be there in about an hour and a half."

As the minutes ticked past, Brett became convinced he wasn't coming. "Something happened. I know it. He won't show up. Typical man!" He finally flopped on the sofa and poured a glass of merlot to both quell his anxiety and feed his growing depression.

A loud knock jolted him and the wine sloshed over the rim of the glass onto the beige carpet. "Shit!" Brett cursed and blotted it up the best he could, finally flipping the cushion over in disgust. "That will do for now!"

Knocking again filled the apartment. "I'm coming! Keep your shirt on!" He bounded down the stairs and stopped just at the bottom, standing away from the door. "Who is it?"

"Room service."

Brett's handsome face broke into a lip-splitting smile and he flung the door open. "It's about time!"

Anthony dropped his bag and took Brett in his arms, kissing him passionately. "God I've missed you!"

Brett relaxed.

AFTERWORD

Raven Hall is a real motel located in the quaint town of New Hope, Pennsylvania. The dining room has won several awards for its cuisine and the new owners have renovated the somewhat rundown rooms to very high standards.

The Golden Nugget Flea Market is also a real place and the vendors there sell everything from salvaged items to expensive antiques.

Peddler's Village is a small town in itself, containing a variety of specialty shops and the famed Cock and Bull Restaurant.

The Lincroft Inn is one of the oldest and most reputable inns in New Jersey. The atmosphere is subdued and the menu limited to fine dining.

The Lambertville House has long been touted as one of the finest restaurants and hotels in western New Jersey.

~ ~ ~

The characters in this work are, of course, fictional. Many are based on myself and others I know. With permission I have used some real names. Bob Burns is a bartender at Raven Hall and gave me permission to use his name, as did the entertainer, Bob Egan. I have enjoyed many meals and celebrations at Raven Hall and continue to do so to this day.

FIN

ABOUT THE AUTHOR

G. Burgess began his writing career as a poet. His work in this genre won him several awards. He then began studying novel writing under mystery author Jane Waterhouse and then under Eileen Evens. He continues to enhance and improve his writing by attending seminars and workshops. He also has a consultant in the police department in Freehold, NJ where he lives. He uses the internet frequently to check for accuracy in his stories. He also continues to read extensively on crime and investigation, focusing on serial, or pattern killers. Raven's Blood is his third novel

G. Burgess is a retired elementary school teacher. He spent nearly 40 years in front of a classroom of eager and willing students in Edison, NJ.